There was a brass plaque mounted on the wall beside the door. The letters on it were authoritative, embossed in stately script:

F. M. HYDE
TAXIDERMIST

There was the sound of metal on metal – a bolt sliding or a tumbler turning out of place – and the door opened halfway on oiled hinges.

For a moment, no one moved. Peter's eyes locked with those of his host. A curious smell drifted through the open door; something vaguely medical that Peter did not recognise. Then the door opened all the way.

'Please come in.'

Also by Liam Smith:

THE WITCHING HOURS

THE PATCHWORK CARNIVAL

HARVEST HOUSE

THE GREATEST SHOW
UNDER THE EARTH

The
Taxidermist

and
Other Gifts

Liam Smith

Copyright © 2022 Liam Smith

Cover art © 2022 huzi79 at fiverr

Illustrations © 2022 Neil Elliott

First printed Anno Domini 2022.

ISBN: 9798840564226

THE TAXIDERMIST AND OTHER GIFTS

An Introduction

Fig 1

We have all given gifts.

We have all received gifts.

Back when I was a boy, I preferred the receiving. I would lie awake in the early hours of a Christmas morning, waiting for a sensible hour to rouse my parents and sister (who was no doubt doing exactly the same thing in her bed in the next-door room), belly fluttering with the excitement of tearing into a fresh pile of presents. When the time came, the unwrapping would be a riot of torn paper and discarded tags and ribbons. Unwrapping presents is like eating sweets; the urge to eat another coming before the first one has even been swallowed.

If you think this sounds materialistic, greedy, or avaricious, I'd agree with you. But I bet you did it too, as a child. As a child, you are driven by the material, the tangible. And we can console ourselves because, sooner or later, we come to prefer the giving of gifts.

I'd always enjoyed making cards for occasions.

When my mum broke her toe, I made her a card in the shape of a foot, with the little toe hinged on a split-pin so that it could rotate around in imitation of the injury. I was twelve at the time, and such a (literally) twisted gift is probably symptomatic of the kind of writer I'd become a little later in life. But it's also symptomatic of the pleasure we can take in giving a gift, a gift that has taken a sacrifice of our time, or money, or effort.

The first story I remember giving as a gift was called *The Christmas Visitor*. Inspiration for the tale struck me as I was getting ready to go to a work event, and I hammered a quick draft out on my laptop before leaving – late – for the company Christmas drinks. It wasn't really written to be a present, but I brushed it up and sent it to a few friends in lieu of sending Christmas cards. A few of them welcomed the gesture, and I enjoyed giving them a unique gift that wasn't just a mass-produced fold of carboard, or a standard-issue notebook or candle.

Stories take time to write, you see. Even the shortest story – and there are two very short ones in this collection – takes not only hours of writing, but also the mental cultivation of an idea that happens for the days or weeks or months before the first draft even begins. I was once given a carved box as a present. It meant a lot because I knew someone had taken a long time making something for me – that instead of going out and having fun, or spending their evenings relaxing in front of the television, they had sacrificed their time to make me happy. And by writing a story for someone, I get to make that same sacrifice, and to give them that same sense of happiness.

The stories in this book were all originally given as gifts. Most of them were given at Christmas, but only one of them takes place at that most wonderful time of the year. Most were given to my nearest and dearest, and they are very happy to regift them for you to enjoy too.

Friends

Firstly, because I know how disappointing it can be to see everyone else unwrapping their presents – here is a present just for you, my lovely reader. I wrote this story in 2016, after my colleagues pointed out a 500-word story competition online. I'd already written *Friends* before realising the competition was for under-eighteens, so it sat on my hard drive for a few years before being pulled out and dusted down for performance at spoken word events, where it always gets a good reception. And now, it is all yours, to enjoy as you like. Unwrap it carefully.

In the Secret Street

There are many regional terms for narrow alleys and passageways – those secret paths that connect larger roads and estates in towns and villages, often overgrown with nettles and offering occasional intriguing glimpses into the gardens that border them. You might be familiar with 'ginnel' or 'twitten' – the latter a Sussex sobriquet, and the one which might be applied to the alleyways that criss-cross the South Coast town where I live and which inspired this story. But 'snicket' is the term favoured in my family, and the one which is employed in this tale.

I love to walk and sometimes even to jog. When I do, I like to dive down snickets and twittens, exploring new secret streets. Once, I found myself on a new cul-de-sac which, at first glance, appeared to have no method of entry or exit other than the alleyway from which I'd just appeared. I wrote *In the Secret Street* shortly after. A story about a mother and son, this tale was given to my own mum for Christmas in 2017.

SIGMA XVI

When my mum received *In the Secret Street* for Christmas, my dad received *Sigma XVI*. Dad got me into progressive rock and I hoped this tale would appeal to him in the same way as spacey prog epics like *2112* and *Cygnus X-1*.

I had always wanted to write something with a sci-fi edge, and the best sci-fi – for me – always had a foot (or tentacle) in the horror genre: usually the weird fiction, body horror or slasher subgenres. Being me, I crafted *Sigma XVI* around the motifs of the gothic horror genre: look out for all the talk of 'chambers' and for the echo of Poe's *Raven* in our lonely protagonist's only confidante.

THE TAXIDERMIST

Here we come to the eponymous tale, whose title is sewn to the front of this sentence-stuffed tome. *The Taxidermist* was my sister Maisie's Christmas present, the third and final of the 2017 yield. It's a stripped-down sort of story, and takes a lot of pleasure in the interplay between its two primary characters. More so, it captures that between-terms feeling, or at least my experience of it, that anyone who has been to university can remember. That, and the bizarre meeting of worlds as a campus-born relationship is framed in a new adult setting – the story draws heavily from my own experience meeting one girlfriend's parents for the first time.

The Taxidermist's stripped-down nature – three characters, one setting – made it ideal material for a short film. When director Chaz Parvez was hunting for a new story to film, I proffered *The Taxidermist*, and he wasted little time in beginning the adaptation. Rory Gauld, one of the actors, described the story as having a *Tales of the Unexpected* vibe, which pleased me no end. At the time of writing, a lot of people have worked very hard on the film. The footage is being edited, and we're all very excited to see the final production.

Rare Cuts

Rare Cuts was a Valentine's present, written for my fiancé and presented to her the year before we were married. We had enjoyed a spell of watching *River Cottage* and broadening our palates with trips to the butcher for less pervasive cuts, and a story drawing from those experiences seemed a fun alternative to a box of chocolates and bouquet of supermarket roses. There are lots of autobiographical elements to the story, but I will leave it to you to guess where the fact ends and the fiction begins.

THE GOBLIN HUNT

I have a wonderful Nanna. She introduced me to my first Stephen King book (*Cycle of the Werewolf*), and recommended me *True Blood* and *Game of Thrones* before I'd even heard of them. But before that, when I was a little boy, Nanna would take me on goblin hunts. A goblin hunt involved a special stick, a woodland trail, and the promise of sticky buns afterward – but let's allow the story to tell you all about it. This tale was of course a gift for Nanna, given Christmas 2019.

UNDER THE OAK

I met Chaz Parvez at an open mic night in Worthing, and jammed along with him on the cajon. We wouldn't cross paths again for two years, when he asked me to review his script for a short horror film. I had never even read a screenplay before, and was woefully unqualified to offer advice on it, so I thanked him for considering my involvement and wished him the best. No problem, he said. But you'll still play drums on the soundtrack?

Psycho Chromatic was the first of Chaz's productions I became involved with, if only marginally. It was only when he was seeking ideas for his second film that I offered him a short story for adaptation – a vignette which was little more than a monologue, written in 2018. *Under the Oak* was adapted as *Beneath the Cedar* after Chaz found a beautiful blue cedar tree, and Holly-Marie Michael delivered a brilliant performance in the lead role, after some names and characters were reconfigured. This is the original tale, as it was when it was given as a gift to Chaz.

Red Christmas

All this talk of gifts has felt rather festive, hasn't it? I don't know about you, but I'm certainly in the mood for a Christmas story.

We've heard of a *White Christmas* – the world's best-selling single, don't you know – and of a *Blue Christmas*, courtesy of the King. You might have heard of a *Black Christmas* – it's a cult slasher flick that predates even Carpenter's *Halloween*. But I hadn't heard of a *Red Christmas* when I wrote this tongue-in-cheek tale in the run-up to Christmas in 2021. My family loved it when they received it on Christmas Eve of that same year, and I hope you enjoy it just as much as they did.

Now – shall we unwrap some of these gifts?

FRIENDS

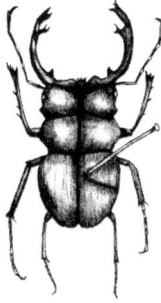

Brian pushed open the front door and stepped through into the living room of his ground-floor flat. His heavy bag scraped as he dragged it over the doorframe, and he stooped to give it a lift, hefting it into the room. He tugged off his coat and hung it on a peg near the door, and in a few minutes he was sat at his table with a cup of tea. It was time to check his Facebook.

Brian knew he did not have many friends in the real world, but that was alright. He had them here at his fingertips. He had favourite friends and he scanned through their pages now, looking at their beautiful faces. Most of his friends were women, but there were a few men too. Brian usually found it easier to talk to women than men, but in his Facebook it didn't matter. He could stare at any of them for as long as he wanted. Sometimes he had fallen asleep with those pages open, waking up to their gaze the following morning.

He'd been with a girl earlier. He'd asked for her name – Megan – before chatting, getting to know her better. Now he needed to add her to his Facebook. Sometimes, when he talked to women – and sometimes men, though not all the time – all Brian really wanted to do was add them, so he could have them all to himself, here in his flat.

Brian drained the last of his cuppa. He'd finished browsing his old friends – now he just needed to add Megan.

He left his empty mug on the kitchen worktop by the sink and opened a door off his living room. It led downstairs. Brian enjoyed having a cellar and had installed a bathtub down there. The cellar was a peaceful place. He filled the tub just shy of the brim, as he usually did after a difficult day. Then he returned to the living room.

Brian heaved the bag over to the top of the stairs, beside his table. He paused, and went to the kitchen to grab a few things. He got back to the living room and dropped to his knees beside the bag. He unzipped it and pulled apart the canvas folds.

Megan's face stared up at him.

Brian returned her smile. Then he got to work.

* * *

Brian washed his hands in the kitchen sink, scrubbing hard with anti-bacterial soap. All taken care of. He dried himself on a tea towel and padded out of the kitchen, his slippers soft on the linoleum floor. He checked through the door to the cellar. The dark shape was visible, floating in the tub, already starting to dissolve. He smiled to himself in satisfaction, and sat himself down at the table.

Removing the skin from the flesh was an art form. Brian opened the pages of his Facebook. The thick leathery pages flipped past, until he reached his most recently added friend. Megan's face gazed back at him.

IN THE SECRET STREET

'Mum. Mum.'

Chloe stirred in her sleep and rolled over. She could feel her dream – something about being on a cruise ship off the coast of Barbados – slip away. She mumbled something and opened her eyes.

'Mum. Are you awake.'

Haha.

'Yes, James.' *I am now, when I could be lying on an ocean liner in the Caribbean. In my dreams.* 'What is it? Why aren't you asleep?'

She pulled herself up onto her elbow and reached for the bedside lamp. The room filled with soft yellow light that made her squint and she slipped on her glasses, thick plastic rimmed things that lived on the bedside table and never left the house.

'Mum. I'm... I'm scared.'

Chloe looked her son up and down. His head hung a little, blonde hair dripping down his forehead.

One arm hung by his side, the other hand held his plush rabbit, Benjamin, by its long ears. It was a hot night. James was wearing pyjama shorts and a thin t-shirt with superheroes on it.

'Did you have a nightmare, James?' Chloe could feel herself teeter on the fence between sleeping and waking. If she could hear about her son's dream soon enough then she could get back to her own before the yellow light and the heat made her too restless to drift back off. 'You want to tell me about it?'

'It wasn't a dream, Mum.' James's spare hand swung over to clutch Benjamin, so that each of the rabbit's ears was secured in its own little bunched fist. 'It really happened.'

'What really happened?' Chloe was losing hope. 'Tell me about it, then you'll feel better.' *And I can get back to Barbados. For the five hours before I have to get up and make your breakfast.*

'It's about a place,' said James. 'Near the school. It's a scary place.' The boy stood there, arms still hanging, head still drooped. He looked like a puppet with its strings cut.

'Why don't you get into bed with me tonight?' Chloe fidgeted with her nightie, pulling it down to her thighs. She hadn't slept naked for eight years or so; not since James had been born. Not that he'd ever made a habit of coming into her room at night, or that she had ever coddled him by letting him sleep with her.

James shook his head.

'I need to tell you,' he said. 'About the scary

place.'

Chloe was still balanced on one elbow. She breathed out through her nose – not quite a huff – and pulled herself up till she was sat against the headboard.

'Alright,' she said, rubbing her eyes behind her glasses. 'Sit down. Don't hold Benjamin's ears like that, they might fall off. Tell me about the scary place. Then we'll figure out what to do about it.'

She glanced at her alarm clock. The red digital display read *11:44*. She'd been asleep for an hour and a half, hitting the sack at ten o'clock after trying out the BBC's new period drama, worn out from a day of calls and typing. James would have been in bed for over four hours. She wondered if he had slept at all in that time, or whether this scary place had been playing on his mind since he'd let her kiss him goodnight and she'd watched him trudge up the stairs to brush his teeth.

The boy clambered onto the bed near her feet and sat cross-legged. His toes were tiny. He set Benjamin in the hollow of his legs and fidgeted with the bunny's ears. Chloe knew the stitching was coming loose on those ears; he would have to stop swinging the toy from them when he carried it around.

'Where's the scary place, then?' Chloe smiled, letting him know that she wasn't scared, that there was nothing to be scared of.

'Near the school,' said James. 'In the houses.'

'The housing estate?'

James's school was a local primary, one of three in their town. It wasn't the closest of the three of them; Chloe drove James to it every day in her old hatchback. But not for the past few weeks; it was the summer holidays.

Lucky things, she thought of the teachers. Six weeks off at the best time of year; what other job allowed that? Here she was, working from home at her phone and her computer, whilst they shot off abroad or just wandered around their homes with nothing better to do.

James was nodding.

'The houses,' he confirmed.

'Is that where you went today? When you went on your bike?'

James nodded again, and Chloe remembered him getting in around four o'clock that afternoon. She'd taken her laptop to the sofa and worked from there whilst James had been out, making use of the quiet living room.

She had watched him push his bike past the French windows, had told him off when he came in for not wearing his helmet. He hadn't argued with her, though usually he would make his excuses. She had expected some attempt at a lie, an *I've just taken it off, Mum*. But she'd forgotten about it as her phone rang and she'd gone back to her report. If James had seemed quiet during their spag bol in front of *The Simpsons*, then she had not been concerned.

'Okay,' she said. 'And you saw something scary. What was it?'

'I'd been there before,' said James. 'I thought it

was fun.'

'Where had you been before?' Chloe was beginning to feel uncomfortable. What if he'd been to a friend's house, watched an episode of *Game of Thrones*?

'The secret street.'

'The secret street?' Chloe looked at her son's face. He was worried, she could see that. A glow of light came from behind her bedroom door: he had left the light on in his room. 'Why is it a secret?'

'Because you can't get in or out,' blurted James. 'Only I've been there. No one else has.'

'Then how did you get there?'

'I walked Crunchie there when I walked round the block.'

Chloe smiled at James.

'That was last week. You weren't allowed to go further than the block.'

'I'm sorry.' James's voice was small. It was devoid of its usual volume and confidence; qualities that had been mentioned to her at more than one parent's evening. In fact, he seemed younger than his years in his fear and uncertainty – he had slipped back into a childish comfort zone where mothers could always offer reassurance. 'I liked exploring.'

The past tense was not lost on Chloe.

'I know you do, my love. Where did you go?'

James frowned, his soft skin wrinkling on his brow.

'I walked down past the play park and I crossed

the long road.'

Chloe nodded. The long road was actually called Tractate Avenue. If James walked back from school with a friend instead of getting a lift with her, he would go via what he called the long road.

'Then where did you go?'

James thought.

'Crunchie wanted to go further. So we did. We went around the houses, near school. We went past the school too.'

'Crunchie wanted to go that way, did he?' Chloe thought of Crunchie, the family whippet, curled up in a basket in the living room downstairs. So this was *his* fault.

'Yes,' said James. He had stopped playing with Benjamin's ears. 'And we looked at the school, over the gate, and it was all empty.'

'Because it's the summer holidays,' said Chloe. 'Everyone's on holiday, even the teachers.' *Lucky things.*

'Yes,' said James again. Now the frown lines were gone. 'Me and Crunchie liked it. It's good not having to go to school.'

'Yes, it is.' Chloe envied her son for a moment. Not a care in the world, really. He didn't have to get up and work, make meals, make money. Life went on for him, no matter what he got up to. What she wouldn't give to have six weeks off; paid, of course. None of this feeling tired all the time, feeling like she was living the same day over and over again, dreaming of holidays with no time to ever take one.

James had been dreaming of course, had gotten himself worked up. Now the fear was gone from his face.

'There now,' said Chloe. 'That's better. There's nothing to worry about. There's no scary places.'

But at those words, the clouds passed back over James's face. His hands went back to his bunny, running its ears through his fists.

'There is, Mummy. I went there. With Crunchie. And... today.'

'Okay,' said Chloe. 'Okay.' She abandoned her last hope of placating her son and shook the last of the sleep from her system. 'Tell me about the scary secret.'

'The secret street.' James's fingers tugged at Benjamin's ears.

'The secret street. Where did you find it?'

'Me and Crunchie left school and walked back along the long road. Crunchie went fast because he knew he wasn't really allowed to have gone so far.'

'I see.'

'And he wanted to go down the little street there. So we did.'

'The little street?' *He's been in someone's garden, hasn't he.*

'The path to the other long road.'

'An alleyway, you mean? A snicket?' Chloe knew what he meant now. The longer parallel roads had little paths connecting them midway along their lengths, so that pedestrians (and cyclists, though they were not meant to) could cut from one street to the next without having to go all the way to the end of the street and around. 'You should be careful there. Naughty people on bikes zoom out of those alleys without looking. And teenagers hang around there. James, I'd rather you didn't go down those little paths.'

'I won't do it again.' James's voice was a whisper. Chloe didn't know if he was heeding her words or thinking of the scary place.

'Okay. Good.' Chloe leaned forwards and rubbed his knee. 'Tell me where you went next. Was it the left or the right path you went through?'

'Left. We went through there and we crossed the other long road.' *Magnus Avenue,* thought Chloe, tracking his route on a map in her mind. 'And we went through the next little path, and the next one.'

Chloe didn't know the names of those streets, but she knew the area roughly. James had been in the housing estate near the town's only secondary school. It was a nice enough place, until you get further from the school. If she was ever to get a mortgage and buy her own place, she could do worse than that neighbourhood.

'Alright. Then where did you go?' *And god, how long was he out the house? Did I not realise at the time?*

'I was there,' said James. 'I was in the secret street.'

Chloe tried to think where this secret street could be; if there were any car parks or properties that James might have stumbled across. She could not think of any.

'But you said there was no way in or out of the secret street,' she said. 'You just wandered down a path to get there. So it can't be that much of a secret.'

'But there were *cars*.' James tugged at Benjamin's ears and Chloe laid a hand on his, stroking at the chubby skin with her thumb. 'There were *cars* but *they* couldn't have gone down the little street to get there.'

'Don't be silly, James.' Chloe soothed him, stroked his hand. 'They must have driven there.'

'*No*. There's *no roads* there, Mummy. There's no roads out of there. The secret street just goes around, and when you go around you end up in the same place you started. Me and Crunchie went round three times. There's another little path on the other side, a snicket-thing, like the one we came through, but nothing else.'

Chloe looked at her son.

'There must have been James. You mean there were houses? There were houses there?'

'Yes. It was a house street. But you can only walk there. There's cars but they couldn't have got there. They couldn't have.'

Chloe thought about what James was saying. That there was some crescent or cul-de-sac in the housing estate that was circular, self-enclosed and inaccessible. But of course, that was impossible. Even if it had been built incorrectly to start with, how would any cars have got there? How would people live there?

Chloe suppressed a shudder that she couldn't quite explain. The secret street must have roads. And even if it didn't, what was the harm? Why had the idea scared James so? She remembered being a child herself, how certain ideas could grow and become more complex than they were. James was just overthinking things.

One day, he wouldn't have time to overthink anything.

'But there were people around, James? There were cars, and people?'

James's lip wobbled and he nodded.

'There you go,' said Chloe. 'Then there must have been a road. Maybe just a small one. A track. That's how people get in there with their cars.'

She had expected this reasoning to calm her son, to simplify the whole idea for him, to reduce it to what it was. But James's mouth turned down and he began to cry, hot wet tears bouncing from his plump cheeks.

'What's wrong?' She pulled herself forwards, rubbed his arms and cuddled him. She could feel twinges of annoyance and quelled them. Kids got worked up about things. She just needed to get to the bottom of this and then James would feel better.

'I thought it was fun.' She felt James's hot blubbery breath against her shoulder as he sobbed. 'I thought it was fun. So I went back.'

'Shhh,' soothed Chloe. 'It's okay. What happened when you went back?'

'I ran around a lot,' said James, and Chloe couldn't stop a smile from twitching her lips. 'I ran around and around and no one stopped me and no cars came because it was my secret street.'

'Was this earlier today, James? Was that this afternoon?'

She felt his head shake against her. His hair was very soft.

'No. Some days ago. I went with Crunchie again. I thought it was fun.'

'Why wasn't it fun anymore?' Chloe picked up Benjamin and nuzzled James's face with it. 'Did someone tell you off for making too much noise?'

His head shook again.

'It *was* okay,' he said. 'But it wasn't today.'

Okay, thought Chloe. *Now we're getting to it.*

'What happened today? Did you go back? On your bike?'

James pulled away from her and took his bunny back. Tears had stained patches on his pyjama top and Chloe could feel damp patches on her nightie. He nodded.

'Yes. Without Crunchie though.'

'Crunchie was home with Mummy this afternoon, wasn't he. Helping me with my work.'

'Yes.' James took a shuddery breath. 'So I went to the secret street. I went through the little paths on the long road to get there. I played on the secret street for ages because the cars don't move and there's no people there.'

'I thought there were people there,' said Chloe. James's mood was infectious and the lateness of the hour sent an involuntary shiver down her spine.

'No,' said James, 'not people. Just cars.'

'Okay, alright.' Chloe smiled at him, though her insides felt peculiar. Outside the bedroom window, the streetlamps went off.

'I played for ages,' repeated James. 'And then... I went to one of the houses...'

He trailed off. Chloe rubbed his knee again, as if easing the delivery of the story.

'You went to one of the houses? A stranger's house?'

James sniffed and nodded, and Chloe bit back a reprimand. He was distressed enough; she would reiterate Stranger Danger to him in the morning.

'I went in the garden because there was no one there,' he said. 'And none of the cars moved. In the secret street nothing moves.'

'Okay,' said Chloe, her hand still rubbing James's knee. She was getting freaked out now, finding it impossible to visualise this still and empty place. How much of this was the product of James's imagination?

'I went up the garden.' James was staring right at her. 'And I looked in the windows. There was nobody inside. So I went through the gate.'

'The gate? To the back garden?'

'Yes. I went through the gate and I went to the garden. There were flowers and grass. And I looked in the big windows and I still couldn't see anyone.'

'What did you do then?' Chloe thought she

knew the answer.

'I went inside. The big window was open a bit and it opened more.'

The French windows, he means, thought Chloe. *He calls our French windows the big windows.*

'It was weird in the house. It was dusty, like when you haven't cleaned my room for ages, but worse. And I looked around and there was a kitchen and settees and it was really quiet. But when I played with the tap in the kitchen no water came out. So I went round the house more and up the stairs and there was no water in the toilet and it didn't flush. And then —'

James's voice was getting quicker, more panicked.

'Then I went in a bedroom and there were people in there *but they weren't people Mummy, they weren't people!*'

James began to cry again and Chloe pulled him close. She had no idea what he meant, but something about those words spooked her, spooked her badly.

They weren't people, Mummy.

What had he seen in there? It sounded like an abandoned house; dusty, the water and electrics cut off. What had been left behind? What were like people but weren't like people?

James sobbed into her shoulder.

Her imagination went wild. Mannequins? Posters? A hat-stand hung with old, moth-eaten coats? It could be nothing; probably was. James had wormed his way into an empty house and his imagination had run away with him, that was all. He knew he was being naughty; he'd been over-excited.

They weren't people Mummy, they weren't people!

James's breathing had slowed. He'd hiccupped a couple of times as Chloe had stroked his hair, and now his sobs had turned into the sighs of sleep. It was as if by describing what scared him he had expelled it from his head, and tiring himself out with tears had led him to drop off in his mother's arms.

Chloe rocked back and lay James down in the bed beside her, pulling the covers up to his chest. His small body rose and fell, and his face was clear of worry.

The light in James's room was still on. Chloe didn't turn it off, only clicked off the bedside light and removed her glasses before laying back beside her son. The glow from James's bedroom helped her eyes to adjust to the gloom, and it was some time before she let herself close them and drift into a shallow, uncomfortable sleep.

They weren't people Mummy, they weren't people!

* * *

The morning came and Chloe eased herself out of bed. The room had become light before five o'clock and she had lain there, sleepless, until six. James was still dozing beside her. He might sleep in this morning. It had been a late night for him.

Chloe wrapped herself in her dressing gown and padded down the stairs and into the kitchen. She got the kettle going and stared out of the kitchen window as the water began to boil. The street outside was quiet. Only a few lights were on in the other houses and no one walked past. Somewhere out of sight cars growled, as commuters began their drives to the nearest cities and towns.

Chloe didn't like the empty street. It felt too much like the place that James had described, the secret street, with its cars that did not move and people that were not —

A car scudded past outside the window and Chloe blinked. Behind her, the kettle's churning peaked and faded. She turned from the window and poured boiling water into a mini cafetiere.

James's story had unnerved her last night. He had seemed so convinced that the secret street was something scary, something impossible. His words had not so much conjured an image in her mind as struck wrong notes in her brain; discordant notes that had discomforted her, made her feel as if something was skewed in the world.

It was easier to shake that feeling in the light of day. Just as a car passing outside her kitchen window had banished her thoughts of emptiness and otherworldliness, so common sense told her that the secret street could not exist.

She plunged the cafetiere and poured herself a strong cup with milk and half a sugar.

35

No, it couldn't exist, and she would have words with James this morning about going into other people's houses, even empty ones.

She scattered some dog food into Crunchie's bowl then made an early start on her emails, replying, forwarding, saving. She supposed she was lucky to have the flexibility to work from home – after all, it allowed her to look after James in the holidays – but it nevertheless felt like an invasion. Home was her sanctuary, and she didn't like to corrupt it with what she normally kept in the office.

James came down the stairs at around eight o'clock, and Chloe set her laptop aside.

'Morning, love.'

'Morning.'

She got up, and James followed her as she headed into the kitchen. She didn't know what to expect from him this morning; if his face would be furrowed with fear or whether it would be carefree and buoyant like it usually was. She poured him some juice from the fridge and put a bowl and a box of Coco Pops on the table. Then she set the kettle boiling for a refill of coffee and watched her son.

He poured himself a bowl of Coco Pops, holding the box in two hands. He didn't eat them with milk. Chloe knew she should be stricter with that. He poked at the bowl with a spoon rather than diving in, and stared straight up at her.

'I'm not as scared this morning,' he said, and Chloe looked back at him.

'No?' she said.

'No,' he said, then munched a spoonful of cereal. 'You'll make it okay.'

'Yes,' whispered Chloe. And then: 'It wasn't just a dream you had, was it James? You weren't even asleep before you came to my room last night, were you?'

James swallowed his mouthful and shook his head.

'Then Mum will make it okay,' said Chloe. 'Of course she will.'

She made her second coffee then went upstairs to change out of her dressing gown.

James was playing with a friend today, a boy from school named Nick. A couple of weeks ago, Nick had come over for a day at Chloe's house. The two boys had played on James's PlayStation until James had got restless and they'd asked to go down to the park. Chloe had let them, pleased that it had been her son who wanted to ditch the electronics and enjoy the sun and fresh air. Now Nick's mum was returning the favour.

She brushed her hair and went back downstairs, dodging James as he scampered up on the way to his room. He seemed back to normal, but Chloe remembered what he'd said in the kitchen.

I'm not as scared this morning.

He wasn't as troubled as he had been last night, but he was still scared of the secret street. But by telling her about it, he had removed most of the weight from his shoulders. Because Mummies could make anything okay. He trusted her to keep him safe, just as she had trusted her parents when she was a little girl.

By the time quarter to ten had come, James was bouncy and excited. She bundled him into the backseat of the car and belted herself into the front, winding the windows down to freshen the stale air that had been baking in the car. It was a ten-minute drive to Nick's house. James had a rucksack on the seat beside him with a selection of toys and video games ready.

Chloe walked him up to Nick's house and said hello to Nick when he opened the door. The two boys bombed into the house, and she smiled at Nick's mum.

'Thank you,' she said. 'I hope he's not too much of a handful.'

'Of course not.' Nick's mother was only a year or so older than Chloe. 'Would you like to come in for a quick coffee? We had the kitchen redone a few weeks ago; I don't think you've seen it yet.'

'I'm sorry. I have to get back to work.' Chloe made a face. 'And I wouldn't like to cramp their style.'

Both women looked up as a thump from upstairs reverberated through the house.

'If you're sure.' Nick's mum's smile was a little more forced as she shut the door.

Chloe reversed out of the driveway and scooted the car along the street. On impulse, she pulled over, slotting the car between a Mini and a white SUV that were parked on the side of the road.

She could see the playing field of the secondary

school from here. Behind that, the redbrick school rose up from the ground, still fresh and new after being built fifteen years ago.

Behind that, the housing estate. And somewhere inside that estate…

The secret street.

If it was real.

Chloe tapped her fingers on the steering wheel. A lady walked a dog past the car.

Don't pretend you didn't have this planned. Don't pretend you've only just thought to check it out.

It was true. She knew she would have to see the secret street for herself; she'd known it since she woke that morning with thoughts of abandoned houses and people that weren't people still roaming around in her head.

'Right,' she said, out loud. 'Let's go then.'

How had James got there? The long road – Tractate Avenue – then left, along the snicket to Magnus Avenue. She would do this properly. She would park on Tractate Avenue and walk from there.

She guided the car through the quiet roads. She wondered if James would have forgotten all about the secret street now that he was playing with his friend. She thought so. She thought it was only when darkness fell that the residual fear began to reactivate, feeding his imagination. Well, it would be easy enough to solve this mystery. She would find this street, take a picture of whatever road or track led into it, and put James's fears *and my own… curiosity…*

to rest.

She turned into Tractate Avenue. The parking signs read 'permit only', but she would only be a few minutes. She couldn't see any traffic wardens.

She heaved herself out of the car. At the very least, this would be a stretch for her legs before she got back to the house and confined herself to the dining table and her laptop for the rest of the day. She left her handbag but pocketed her phone, ready to take any pictures that she could show to James.

The snicket was capped by two staggered sets of rails; a miniature chicane to deter cyclists from entering . Chloe trotted around them and began down the little path.

It was the length of two back-to-back houses and their gardens. The surface of the path was uneven, and Chloe side-stepped a dog mess that had been dolloped in the middle of it. She emerged on the other side, on Magnus Avenue.

The next alleyway was dead opposite her, and she waited for a Royal Mail van to pass before crossing the road. It was a lovely day, warm and sunny, but the heat itched at Chloe and she couldn't let herself relax. James had been scared – that was the thing. He hadn't just made his story up: it was rooted in something real, something that had frightened him. Chloe was apprehensive, and her worry for her son translated to a fluttering in her stomach.

She passed through the second alleyway and

onto the next road. She didn't know its name, and the only signs must have been at the top and bottom of the street. It ran parallel to Tractate and Magnus and looked of a similar length.

She crossed the road again. The next snicket was longer, and curved round the back of a garden. A monkey puzzle tree towered over the right angle, spikey arms blocking the sun for a second. Dark green weeds poked through the piney-smelling fence panels. The path angled again, back on itself, and Chloe found herself on another street.

How many paths had James taken on his explorations? Was this the secret street?

She looked around. A few cars were parked up, but no people roamed the pavements. But that wasn't unusual – it was a weekday. Most people would be at work.

She stepped out of the shadow of the snicket and onto the street proper. The houses weren't as nice as the ones on the previous two roads and certainly weren't as well maintained as those on Nick's estate. Some of the walls were stained with grime and a grubby Tiny Tikes car had been left on its side in a front garden.

She began to walk up the street – in a rough northerly direction. This was a nice enough town, and Chloe didn't feel endangered by walking in this area. It was just a bit grottier than the area she lived in; all towns had their nicer and nastier parts.

It did seem quiet here. She could hear cars

vrooming somewhere nearby, but nothing moved in her vision. So still; so strange –

A cough from a nearby garden. A chunky man in tracksuit bottoms and a hoodie looked at her over a low garden wall as he ambled over to his front gate. Chloe gave him a slight smile and continued on her way.

Then there were people after all. There was nothing untoward about this place. Only…

She been expecting something circular. A crescent or a ring of houses. What had James said? He'd run around it, several times. This couldn't be the secret street.

As if to compound this realisation, a car rumbled into life behind her and slid away. Chloe watched as it drove to the bottom of the street then turned left, down a clearly visible junction.

Where had James got to? There wasn't another snicket, was there..?

Chloe looked over the road.

A small track cut a path between two rows of terraced houses. A red-ringed signpost by its entrance had a small bicycle printed on it. The post was slightly bent and the round sign had been twisted around, so it hadn't been obvious until she'd gotten closer. There were no chicanes at the entrance.

Chloe looked both ways before crossing the road.

The path here was badly maintained, gravelly and weed-choked, and her boots slipped a little on the loose stones. It was dark as well; the bulk of the houses on either side blocked out the sunlight even at this time of day. The brickwork of the houses gave way to high fences and Chloe couldn't see over the tops into the gardens on either side. But then, all of a sudden:

She was there. The secret street.

There was no doubt about it; this was it. It was just like she had imagined when James had told her about it. She stood at the mouth of the alleyway and looked about.

The road curved away to her left and right; it was, as far as she could tell, a circle. At the centre of the circle, directly opposite from her, were two back-to-back semi-detached houses, joined by their rear gardens. There were gardens in front too. More houses, some semis, some detached, bordered the circumference of the street. Odd cars were parked on driveways and on the road.

Chloe took a few steps forward. It was very quiet here; she couldn't even hear the traffic or activity from adjacent streets. Not a vehicle moved, not a soul could be seen. It was almost unsettling.

But it's not, Chloe told herself. *It's just a quiet day on a secluded crescent.*

Time to find a road, then.

She began to walk anticlockwise around the circle.

All the houses were slightly different, she noticed. Some were redbrick, some were yellow. Some had mock Tudor fronts, others had garages, some had chimney stacks, some had ponds. It was like a city planner had stipulated no building could be the same. Chloe might have found it charming but for the absolute stillness of the place. There wasn't even any birdsong in the air.

She was about a quarter of her way round the circle now. She could see back to the path she'd come from: there was no *no-cycling* signpost on this side. When she looked forward, she could see there was a similar path at the opposite side of the circle. Neither track was large enough to admit a car. She kept walking, her steps slow and small.

What a strange place, she thought. The windows of the houses around her stared down impassively. A car on her left caught her eye and she paused to stare at it. *Something's not right...* She frowned and went on her way. She reached the second secret path and stared down it. It looked much the same as the first had.

'Hmmm.'

Chloe's voice sounded very tiny, and she repeated her exhalation a little louder. There was no one around to hear her talking to herself. She passed another car, and could not shake the feeling that she was missing something obvious.

Clever boy, she thought suddenly. *It's one thing to notice that's there's no road to a place, but another to ask how the cars got in here.* But surely there was a road; surely she was missing something. A dirt track behind a garage that gained access to the secret street, a slipway between two houses. She just hadn't seen it yet.

Could a small car get down one of the snickets? A Smart Car? These cars were all too big; estates, saloons…

Just a minute. She looked at the closest car. *What make is it?*

There's no badge on the boot of the car.

Chloe strode to the front of the vehicle and checked the bonnet. Nothing. She looked the car up and down. Nothing to indicate the brand. She scrutinised the car. The headlights looked misty. She couldn't see any bulbs behind the thick glazing.

She looked around her. There was no one to be seen. She walked up to the driver's side door and peered in, placing her hand against the glass.

Dashboard, steering wheel, gear stick…

But no handbrake. And the speedometer was a blank white circle, with no arrow or even numbers on its face.

What kind of car was this?

A fluttering in Chloe's belly rose up to her throat. What was this place? This car was like… like… a toy, or something! Like something James would play with; a model, with no close detail.

'Where am I?' she asked, and when her voice seemed too small, she repeated it. 'Where am I?'

There was no answer.

So she would get one.

Chloe marched up to the door of the nearest house and rang the bell. Flowers in the garden dipped their heads in a slight breeze, yet even that seemed suddenly sinister to Chloe. Where were the bees, the insects? It was a summer's day!

There was no answer at the door, so Chloe rapped on it with her knuckles. She wondered which house James had been inside, and stepped back reactively as she thought of his words.

They weren't people, Mummy!

No one answered the door.

'Fine,' she muttered. She marched back along the garden path and opened the gate of the house next door. This house was painted white and was striped with black beams. Its windows were scored with diamond patterns and its roof was perfectly tiled.

The door looked oaken and was studded with small iron knobs. Chloe banged hard with a knocker and waited. There was no reply here either. She looked around her.

James did it, she thought. Then: *no! You're an adult. You can't get away with…*

With trespassing. With breaking and entering.

It wasn't like the door would be unlocked anyway.

Chloe looked around her. She was alone in the secret street.

She reached out to the door's large, ornate handle, and took it in her fist. The door opened at the slightest push.

'Hello?'

Chloe bent her head into the doorway. It was gloomy in the house; there were no lights on.

'Is there anyone there?'

She paused, and then took a step inside.

She was in a front porch. The walls were papered with patterns and a line of coat hooks stood empty at her side. She pulled the door to behind her and went further into the house. She went to open a closed oak door and then pulled her hand back as if scalded. What if there was someone inside?

Well, I'm already in the house.

Nonetheless, she let the door be, and continued.

She entered a large dining room with a country-style kitchen against one wall. She looked around her. There were no signs of life, but the dining room table was made up with six place settings, as if waiting to be used. Chloe approached the table. It was covered in a thin but obvious layer of dust; just as James had described. Remembering her son's words, she made for the kitchen. She reached for a brass tap and twisted. Nothing came out. The white butler sink below it was stain-free, but grey with a thin lining of dust.

What were the chances that she and James had stumbled into the same house on the secret street? Slim. There were dozens of homes out there. Then they must all be abandoned. Why leave the place laid as if for a banquet?

Chloe felt on edge. Her pulse beat in her throat. She wasn't supposed to be here. And yet, how could she leave without exploring further?

The stairs did not creak as she climbed them.

It was like she'd stepped into a film set; a pretence of reality. This place didn't seem real. She remembered a film she'd once seen where a whole village, complete with houses and roads and kitchens and furniture, had been built to test bombs on. That must have been like a film set within a film set. That was how she felt now.

She reached the top of the stairs. It was gloomier up here; none of the lights in the house were on and there were no windows on the landing. None of the doors up here were open.

'Hello?' she tried again. She expected no reply, and received none. She walked along the landing and opened the door at the far end.

A bathroom. She didn't try to flush the toilet.

Perhaps this was a film set; a little one built in the middle of a housing estate years before for some dated ITV drama, all forgotten about. That was the only explanation. Wasn't it?

She left the bathroom.

James had been right about everything; had described everything as it had been. It felt so unnatural here, although there must be a rational explanation.

But no – that's not what had scared him now, was it?

Mummy!

And Chloe knew she could not leave without looking inside at least one of these rooms.

She tiptoed to the closest door and pushed it gently forwards. It whushed on the thick carpet and Chloe peeked inside.

A four-poster bed, curtains drawn back. Empty. Wardrobes, a vanity unit.

No one inside.

Okay.

Next room.

Tip toe. Push.

The same bed, curtains pulled back. The same furniture, dressing table. Different wallpaper. A doll's house rested on a table under the window.

No one inside.

Nothing to fear.

Chloe's steps grew bolder. She pushed the next door without caution and stepped inside

Oh god –

She clapped a hand to her mouth to stopper a scream of surprise.

'I'm sorry,' she gasped, 'I just came in to – to…'

She trailed off. The figure at the window didn't move.

'I'm sorry,' she repeated. Her heart was hammering like a fire alarm, throbbing in her ears. 'I didn't know anyone was…'

She stepped inside the room.

They weren't people, Mummy!

It wasn't a person. She walked up to the figure, breathing shallow, spine crawling as if she were being watched. She pulled the curtain away from the window, spilling light into the room.

It was a doll. A life-size female doll. Its eyes

49

were two shining discs of glass, its skin hard plastic. Its limbs were frozen into a pose, one arm raised as if waving a greeting, the other down by its side. It was dressed in a skirt and blouse with a fur coat around its shoulders.

A film set, thought Chloe. *It's a dummy left over from filming. A mannequin.*

She stared at the figure and it stared back. Chloe hated it but did not want to turn her back on it. It scared her. Just as it, or one like it, had scared James.

Her heart thrummed in her ears. She backed away from the figure, nearly screamed when she collided suddenly with the wall. She closed the door behind her as if she feared the dummy would give chase, and then scrambled down the stairs.

She ran through the huge kitchen, past the dusty dining table. She bolted for the front door, throwing it wide open and pelting out onto the street.

For a moment she was disorientated; the circular shape of the secret street seemed eternal, alien. It took her a moment of breathless spinning to locate the path she'd come through to get there. And then she looked at the semi-detached houses in the centre of the road.

The roof was gone from one of the houses.

Chloe gaped at the house. She'd heard nothing. Had it collapsed? Where was the rubble? Where was the destruction?

But there was nothing. The roof had vanished, as if someone had reached down and plucked it away, leaving the upper storey open.

She thought of the house she'd just been in. She thought of the bedrooms, and what was inside one of them. Not the final bedroom, not the mannequin in there.

The second bedroom.

The doll's house.

She looked back at the central house. There were no rafters lancing into the sky, no signs that there had ever been anything laid on top of the walls.

Chloe's legs were running before her brain had even begun to instruct them to do so. She sprinted for the alleyway even as a shadow fell across her, darkening the ground as if a thick cloud had stationed itself in front of the sun. She did not dare look up; not because it would slow her down but because she did not want to see whatever had made that shadow, whatever god-sized thing had erected its toy in the middle of a small-town housing estate.

She crashed into the fence of the snicket, bouncing off and throwing herself down the alleyway, skidding on the loose gravel and erupting from the other side of the path into the middle of the road.

A car honked its horn and swerved to avoid her. Chloe didn't even move. A hand flew out of the passenger window and gesticulated at her, but she didn't see it. Now she raised her eyes to the sky, irresistible to the lure of what she might see.

There was nothing. Nothing but white whisps of cloud on a blue sky.

Chloe stumbled back onto the pavement, neck craned.

What had she expected? A chubby arm, reaching from the heavens to move its playthings about?

She didn't know what she had expected.

She put her hands on her knees, breathing hard, and looked down at the ground. A few ants crawled on the warm tarmac. She looked up again. Still nothing.

After a minute or two, she began to walk. Back through the twisting snicket, past the towering monkey puzzle. Back to Magnus Avenue, then Tractate Avenue. There was a parking ticket on her car. Fifty pounds, or twenty-five if paid within a fortnight. She climbed into the car, sat for a moment with the windows down.

Her phone rang, and she glanced at the screen. It was work. She ignored it for a moment, then started the car. In ten minutes, she was back at her house.

Tonight, she would talk to James about Stranger Danger, and about where he was allowed to play. And that he mustn't *ever* go back to the secret street again.

Sigma XVI

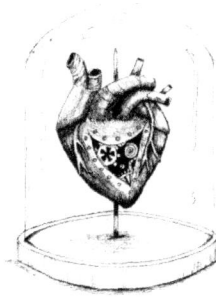

The astronaut came to with a gulp of air so large he felt he must have torn a leak in his lungs. There was no way they could contain so much air. But his body craved oxygen, and he managed to fill himself to the brim before exhaling.

Then the nausea hit.

His eyes were still bleary from the stasis and he groped outside the pod, desperately holding down the contents of his stomach with just-woken muscles. A flat, silver shape edged into his vision and he reached for it. The shape – it hovered half a metre above the floor– reached out a pair of arms of its own. There was a bio-bin held in its hands.

With a grunt of relief, the astronaut vomited. The silver shape watched with smooth black lenses and softly flashing red lights.

* * *

'Where are we?'

The astronaut was dressed now, the engineered fabric of his thermo-suit baggy after his time in the pod. He slumped in the cockpit's only chair, still pale. His body ached, and he could feel the slight overcompensation of the ship's gravity simulators fighting against his muscles. A migraine pulsed behind his eyes.

'Solar system designated Sigma XVI.'

The silver robot glided to the cockpit's console. The bio-bin was gone; emptied into the ship's waste processor and decontaminated. Now the robot's claw-like hands manipulated the switches and buttons of the control panel, the whir of its electronics just audible in the silence of the craft. As it twisted one dial through several rotations, its claw turned with it, rotating completely three times. The effect was wholly inorganic.

'How long was I out?'

'Thirty-two years, one month and nine days.' The robot's words came from somewhere within its saucer-shaped body. Its voice had been donated by one of the engineers that had built it. Its timbre was soft and female, its cadence carefully patterned after real speech. This made it easier to believe it was a sentient being. 'We have travelled thirty-two light years since leaving the system designated Sigma XV.'

'I'm feeling every one of them.' The astronaut sighed and rubbed his eyes. 'Any communications?'

'I have compiled a report on all incoming

transmissions. No qualified signals from alien sources. No received transmissions from home.'

Home. The astronaut guessed that word had been chosen on purpose, to make the robot seem more sympathetic. Home was a long way away. But that other word still gave him a shiver of excitement.

Alien.

For that was the point of the mission, was it not? To find something else, anything else, in the endless universe? And what would that thing be, if not an alien?

The astronaut looked up. The roof of the cockpit was punctured by three large, circular windows. The polymer that made up the glazing was inches thick to separate him from space but, still, the yawning blackness on the other side seemed very close and very powerful.

The scientists at home reasoned that there must be other life in the universe. How could there not be? There were more stars in the universe than all the words ever uttered, each with the potential to harbour life in the habitable zone of its solar system. The universe was infinitely large, more expansive than anyone could comprehend. There must be other life – it was just a matter of finding it.

'Any word from the fleet?'

The astronaut closed his eyes and lay back in the pilot's seat. He was in pain. The stasis was not a natural state and his body rejected its effects.

'No word from the fleet.' The robot's words

didn't have any of the empathy of a real companion, even with its carefully designed voice.

Maybe if they had really wanted to make a robot that looked like us, they wouldn't have made it a saucer with arms.

'I estimate the closest craft to be over one thousand light years from our current position.'

'Just what I wanted. Some alone time.' The astronaut glanced at the robot. It did not reply. 'I hope Omega doesn't find anything first. Never could stand her. How many planets in the habitable zone?'

The robot engaged with the control panel, pressing buttons and booting up a screen in the console's centre. A map of the current solar system appeared.

'One planet matches our requirements for intelligent life. Two other terrestrial planets may provide conditions for adapted strains of life.'

'Three to check then.' The astronaut stood and stretched, peering through the middle porthole. Even at this distance, the nearest star seemed huge, dwarfing any other bodies in the solar system. 'I hope if – when – we find something, it's not just some plant. Or worse: a bacterium.'

The robot did not respond.

'I know it's still life, but…' The astronaut looked back out of the window, at the yawning gulf of space. 'A single-celled organism doesn't capture the imagination like a real alien, does it? Not so good for conversation either.'

'We are searching for all forms of life on this

mission.' The robot adjusted a dial and the map of the planetary system disappeared from the monitor.

'I wonder what they would look like…' The astronaut ignored his companion. 'If they would walk, or fly, or swim. How many legs they've got – or how many tentacles, or roots. Or maybe they would slide along in a puddle of their own slime…'

'I must initiate recharge sequence,' announced the robot. 'Course is set for the habitable zone. Automatic controls are enabled. Recharge session will last seventeen hours.'

The astronaut watched the robot disengage from the console and glide back through the cockpit. There were two sets of doors at the rear of the room, each comprising a pair of sliding metallic panels. One was linked to the rest of the ship, and the other door was sealed to him. The word *SIGMA* was printed across the sealed door.

The robot reached the door and plugged its claw into a panel on the wall. There was a mild whirring sound and the door opened, splitting apart down its middle to admit its guest. The robot rotated and reversed into the space.

'Goodnight, Sig.' The astronaut peered after the robot. The walls of its chambers were lined with further monitors and buttons. 'Whatever you get up to in there,' he muttered, as the doors slid shut.

* * *

The astronaut supposed he was old. He had not asked the robot exactly how long he had been suspended since the mission began, but from the distance they had travelled he knew he was living beyond his years, if one measured time in such a linear way.

But one did not. Time passed differently aboard the *Sigma*. It was revelations about the inseparable nature of time and space that had renewed the people's interest in space exploration and in the possibility of other life in the universe.

The astronaut wondered if one of the other exploration craft had found any signs. They had all launched within the space of six months or so: twenty ships, each with its own course plotted, spoking out into the observable universe. Each carried a Sentience Detection Aide – the astronaut wondered if all the Aides had female voices like his.

Those first weeks on the *Sigma* had been incredible. He had been in space before – posted to the national space station twice, served on a team that evaluated moon habitability potential – but had never, ever been so far from home.

The ship's computer had informed him when they had passed out of orbit and into deep space, but he thought he would have known anyway. The sense of scale was almost overwhelming. The absolute blackness of the universe, invisible and yet so immediate, pushed right against the walls and windows of the ship. The millions of stars – and, here, he could truly believe there were millions. With no light from the planet's surface to bleach out his view, the sky was alight with them, too many for him to count, smattered and clustered and glittering on the sable canvas of the galaxy.

There was a sense of responsibility; a great one. But that was not why he had volunteered for this enterprise. No – it was the knowledge that he would be part of something monumental. No – not monumental, that was too small a word, too grounded, too entrenched on the planet's surface. This was the most important expedition ever mounted, and he was at its forefront. He didn't care if history remembered his name or not. He only cared that he was seeing parts of the universe that nobody else ever had and if – when – some sign of life was detected, it was his honour to see it first.

The paths of the fleet took them all in different directions. Procedure dictated that each astronaut place him or herself into stasis once a steady course was set through space, leaving the maintenance of the craft to its SDA. But this would have meant sacrificing all communication within two weeks of launch. He had kept a line through to Omega for nearly a month, their brief messages flashing in green text on the console's monitor, getting less and less frequent as the ships travelled farther and farther apart.

When no reply came at all, the astronaut had entered the cryo chamber.

* * *

In time, they reached the system's habitable zone.

The astronaut turned at the sound of bleeping. The doors to the SDA's chamber slid open, splitting the word *SIGMA* into two. The saucer-shaped robot emerged, gliding towards the console.

'Morning Sig.'

His little joke. There were no mornings in space.

'Recharge completed.' The robot reached an arm to the control panel and plugged a claw into a port on the system. Its soft red lights flashed green.

'I always have to go when I first get up.' The astronaut smirked, and the robot did not reply.

I don't think it likes me, he thought. *Wait, of course it doesn't. It's not alive. It can't feel.*

This is the reason we put ourselves in stasis, he mused. *Not just to keep us alive. To keep us from thinking too much.*

'What's the planet?' he asked out loud.

'Planetary body designated Sigma XVI-4.' The robot disengaged from its terminal and began to manually type at the buttons on the panel. The monitor faded into life and the astronaut watched as it loaded its previous display: the diagram of their current system. As the robot tweaked the controls, the display zoomed in on the fourth planet from its star. 'Located on the edge of the habitable zone. Initial scans show no surface water but chances of frozen reservoirs beneath the surface.'

'How do we know they need water to survive? Just because we – well, I – do?' The astronaut looked at the robot. He knew why. He hadn't passed a stringent selection process or rigorous training programme to lose all his knowledge in stasis. In terms of mental and physical condition he was at his peak – all the explorers were. They were potential ambassadors for the species. He just wanted to see if the robot would reply.

There was silence for a moment. Then:

'Secondary scans show signs of ice beneath the planet's surface.'

The monitor refreshed, showing a three-dimensional render of the planet they were approaching.

It didn't answer my question. The astronaut looked at the robot as its claws extended, retracted, swiped and rotated across the console. *It ignored me. It should have answered my question. That's what it's there for.*

'Entering orbit now.' The robot paused. 'Manual navigation required.'

The astronaut blinked. The robot did not move.

'What's so difficult about this one?' The astronaut sat up in the pilot's seat and pulled himself towards the controls. The system of joysticks, buttons and switches were provided for tasks that required a more organic input than the SDA could provide. Gut instinct, he called it. One thing that artificial intelligence couldn't be programmed with.

'Manual navigation required.'

The astronaut looked across at the hovering saucer, but it said nothing more.

'Alright.'

He activated the manual controls. Entering orbit was not difficult; the only challenge was to meet the altitude requirements to launch a probe down to the planet's surface, whilst remaining clear of any dangerous elements in the atmosphere that could damage the craft.

'It's done.' The astronaut flipped ship back to automatic controls and stood up. It had been the work of minutes, but he had enjoyed the sense of responsibility that had been his for that short term. 'Let's get a probe down there.'

He crossed to the doors at the back of the cockpit and prodded the panel to open them. The corridor beyond formed a kind of spine for the craft; rooms branched off on either side. To his right were his own quarters, containing a bed and a set of shelves for his few effects. The robot's charging chamber was opposite, though there was no access to it from the corridor.

There was a kind of refectory on the left of the spine – little more than space for a vending machine – as well as a plant room, which contained the decontamination machine and recycling and filtration systems whilst doubling as a bathroom. The cryo chamber was at the rear of the craft and he headed there now. The ceilings were low, and he felt the roof brush his head as he walked. For a moment he felt something like vertigo as he considered how close his body was to the gulf beyond. But it passed, and he reached for the panel that opened the chamber door.

As well as the cryo pod and its network of tubes, tanks and controls, this place housed the qualification probes. Additionally, it housed the ejection gear that would launch a probe down onto the planet below.

The astronaut saw the shadow of his Sentience Detection Aide appear on the smooth metallic floor next to him.

'Alright Sig.' He crouched to boot up the ejection gear and looked back at the robot.

'All systems active and prepared for launch.' The robot hovered.

'Gets you feeling maternal, does it?' The astronaut pointed at the battery of probes. Each was a shiny saucer, only a little smaller than the SDA itself. The arms of the probes were all retracted for storage and transportation, and they were stacked up in magazines of ten. So far, the *Sigma* had launched forty-five probes. 'Are you sad to see another one escape the nest?'

The robot did not reply.

'No sense of humour.' The astronaut dispensed one probe from its magazine and hefted it to the ejection chamber. It was perhaps half a metre in diameter and surprisingly heavy. Whilst the SDA was packed with complex software to help run the ship, the probes were burdened with hardware – sensors, scanners and sample tubes. 'And now: my favourite part.'

He sealed the chamber and glanced at a small screen to its left. The probe remained visible behind a transparent polymer shield.

'Activate probe.' The astronaut muttered as he entered a familiar sequence on the control pad, and the probe levitated an inch or two from the floor of the ejection chamber. 'And… fire!' He thumbed a final button and the floor of the chamber dropped away. There was a slow flash of white light as the saucer was launched – and then the chamber was empty.

'All do —'

The astronaut stopped short as he stood up and found himself face to face to with the robot. It was hovering at his eye-level; he'd almost collided with it. 'Sig,' he said. 'Let's keep this relationship professional.'

The robot retreated.

'Probe launched. Estimated landing time is…'

The astronaut shrugged as he watched the saucer glide away. All machines had their little glitches.

* * *

They stayed at the planet for twenty orbits. The ship scanned for signs of life and found none. The qualification probe, down on the planet's surface, scanned for any anomalous elements; anything out of place that suggested the organic interaction. If it found none during their brief stay, it would continue to scan in their absence. They would be able to communicate with the probe up to a distance of five light-hours away.

The astronaut analysed the data that poured from the ship's computers. He could see the planet through the portholes in the cockpit. Now that they were within orbit, it filled his vision. The planet – designated Sigma XVI-4 – was a reddish-brown colour. It did not appear to have any plant life, or any polar ice regions. It just looked like desert. Data confirmed the planet had no atmosphere and his hopes of finding something here, already minute, reduced to nothing.

The probe would first circumnavigate the planet around its equator. Then it would cut below the planet's surface to explore the ice reservoirs. That would take weeks; the probe would have to re-emerge periodically to recharge by the light of the local star.

It would continue to beam any data back to the *Sigma* that it collected, even after the craft left the planet's orbit. Information would be qualified by the ship's computers and by the SDA before the astronaut bothered to look at it.

* * *

The stasis was a strange thing. Or perhaps it was the nature of this mission. The astronaut felt tired, all the time. It wasn't that his body wasn't fuelled – the nutrient-rich recycled foods from the vending machine saw that he was well-nourished – but more that it wasn't... charged. It wasn't fully awake.

Perhaps it was because he was old. For how long had he stayed in that pod? He was under no illusion that his slumber was measured in centuries, not years. He was ancient but alive, artificially alive.

Perhaps it was because he was alone. There was nothing but space all around him. The sky might be full of stars but there was so much distance between those stars. And space itself... It wasn't stuff. It wasn't made of anything. It was an absence of stuff. An emptiness of things. That was almost its saving grace. How could he be afraid of that gulf when it wasn't made of anything – when it wasn't really there?

The last time he had felt a flicker of energy had been when he had brought the craft manually into orbit – at least he had felt needed. Important, even.

The astronaut scrolled back through the communications log. There were many radio signals – bursts of interference from the collapse of stars, waves from the rotation of a nearby ringed planet – but no messages. Not since that final message from Omega. He'd replied to it. He wondered if she had ever received it – whether they were both now circling in strange galaxies, wondering which of them had been the last to read the words of the other.

'But who needs her when I've got you?'

The astronaut looked over at the robot. It was plugged into the console and did not respond.

'You're getting awfully quiet, Sig. Are you bored of my company?'

The saucer's lights flashed amber around the flat black lenses of its optical processors.

'Data indicates no sign of life on planet designated Sigma XVI-4.'

'That's not what I asked. Come on now. We're friends, aren't we? I've spent more time with you than anyone else in the whole universe! Keep me company.'

The astronaut waited for it to reply. He wondered what software was at work inside it, computing an answer that it had no emotive response to.

'We have been together for six thousand years, eight months and five days.' The robot's light stopped flashing and remained a steady red.

'Wh—'

The astronaut paused, his mouth open.

'We have spent six thousand years, eight months and five days together.'

The astronaut fell silent. There was nothing he could say to describe the feeling that had hit him in that moment – some mix of fear, grief, self-pity and hopelessness. He had never calculated the length of the mission, never construed his age from the expedition statistics. He had not wanted to know. Knowing made the truth tangible – that everyone at home that he had shared his life with, even the members of the agency that had launched *Sigma*, had passed away many years ago.

'Why tell me that?' The astronaut looked now at the robot. It hovered, still, lights a constant red. 'Why tell me that?'

'You asked how long we had been together in the universe.' The lights turned green. 'I answered your question.'

'I didn't...' He hadn't asked it that, had it? He hadn't wanted to know. He couldn't remember what he had said when teasing the robot. 'Don't tell me that again, alright? Don't tell me how long we've been together. Don't tell me how long it was since we launched. Don't tell me how old I am.'

'Logged.' The robot turned back to the console. The astronaut stared at it for minutes after it had spoken.

They'd known what this expedition involved. He, Omega, all of them, knew. Their cryogenically lengthened lives would extend far beyond those of anyone at home. The team that had masterminded this exploration would be long gone – they had not expected results in their lifetimes. This mission was for the benefit of the planet, not for a small clique of scientists. Still, to know he had been alive for thousands of years...

Would the planet be the same when he returned? So much progress would be made in those millennia, so much change. Perhaps the space programme had already been halted. Perhaps if he were to return, everyone would mistake him for an alien. Would they even know what he had done – what sacrifice he had made?

These were thoughts that the astronaut had kept sealed in his head throughout the mission. He was intelligent, he had always been able to conceive of these concepts, but he had known the danger they represented. Ruminating in this way would drive him to insanity.

He looked at the robot again. Why? Why had he led it to that – to telling him how old he was? It should have been programmed differently – kept that kind of information in that locked chamber at the back of the room.

He glanced at that chamber door. *SIGMA* printed across it.

He wondered if any of the other nineteen explorers had realised how old they were – if their SDAs had informed them. Had it driven any of them crazy? He could feel the threat of that now and sensed he needed to stop thinking. He wished he could empty his mind of thoughts and questions and uncertainty, until it was as empty as that vacuum of space beyond the walls of his ship.

Maybe a nap in the cryo pod would settle his brain.

* * *

The astronaut stood over the cryo pod. It looked like a coffin.

It was a white box, smooth and rounded like a bathtub, and its lid was open at just over ninety degrees. There were tubes leading in and out of the pod; their open mouths yawned over the cavity itself. These would supply the pod with fresh fluids, constantly removing, refreshing and replenishing the liquid his body would be suspended in. The lid had a porthole in it. The astronaut supposed this was to reduce the effect of claustrophobia as it descended over the operative within.

He had felt claustrophobia once upon a time. Once, the thought of space made him feel it. He had felt trapped, bound by the massiveness of it, the pressure. But with acclimatisation came release. Now he felt no claustrophobia, no agoraphobia. One by one, his feelings were leaving him.

He hoped a period of dormancy in stasis would help to push these thoughts from his head, like a good night's sleep helps relieve a fever. He knew he did not dream in the pod, or at least, could not remember dreaming, and his memories of exploring previous solar systems with the SDA were fuzzy in his mind. Hopefully these memories would be too. Hopefully, he could erase the uncertainty he had felt in Sigma XVI.

His hand hovered over the activation button. Once engaged, the pod would begin to fill with the fluids that would keep his body alive beyond its years. They were cold. He remembered that. The ship's computers would hand over control to the robot as the pod prepared for his interment.

Until he pressed that button, the robot did not know what he was planning.

It would try and stop him, wouldn't it? They had not finished exploring the habitable zone yet – his work was not done.

But it doesn't need me. The astronaut glanced back at the door to the cryo chamber, as if his gaze could penetrate the metal and polymer surfaces and see through to the cockpit. *It's learned how to do everything itself.*

He thought to when they had entered the orbit of the planetary body designated Sigma XVI-4, when he had last felt needed.

It didn't need me then, he thought. *But it knew I was feeling uncertain. It knew to make me feel important.*

Could that be true? Could it have let him enter orbit just to pretend he was still needed, still necessary?

Perhaps. Hadn't the robot begun to pick and choose when and how it replied to him? It was programmed to be his aide – to answer questions when asked. But wasn't it now analysing his remarks, filtering those that were flippant or rhetorical? Was it now selectively answering him, not with clear answers, but with a politician's statements and half-truths?

The astronaut's gaze hadn't moved from staring at the door, and for a strange moment he felt a twinge of dread, as if the robot could penetrate his mind and download his thoughts for analysis.

Nonsense. And yet, the robot was more aware than ever. It was more artificially intelligent now. Could it... Could it *think*?

The astronaut did not move for a whole minute. When he did, it was to turn back to the cryo pod.

That was enough. Let the dreamless repose of stasis grant him some relief.

His thumb hovered over the activation button.

Was it safe? Was he safe, asleep, with the robot onboard?

The pause stretched on.

Of course he was. This was all speculation, wasn't it? Just his starved imagination; the isolation of space manifesting as paranoia. He'd survived six thousand years, hadn't he? Just let the pod take it from here.

He stared into the coffin a moment more, then reached for the button.

A green light flashed around the room before his finger landed. It pulsed on and off, on and off; an alarm.

No: green wasn't an alarm. It was an alert.

Probably just some anomalous signal; a strange wave emanating from a local comet.

Unless...

The astronaut left the cryo chamber and headed for the cockpit.

'What's up, Sig?'

He sat in the pilot's seat and activated the

monitor. Here the green light limited itself to a flashing electronic bulb on the control panel.

'Qualification probe has encountered an anomaly on planet Sigma XVI-4.' The robot was plugged into the console.

'What kind of anomaly? That's the red planet?'

'The anomaly is a terrestrial object with radiation levels that do not match any other object so far discovered on the planet's surface.'

'You mean it's come from another planet?'

'Data indicates it is a possibility.'

The astronaut looked out of the portholes, but the planet was not in his view and, at this distance, would appear as nothing more than a large, bright star.

'Could it be a meteorite? A recent one?'

'It is possible. Awaiting further data.'

The astronaut sat back. For moments, his imagination had run wild. He'd envisioned some futuristic outpost, something made by subterranean inhabitants who surfaced periodically from their underground cities. But his excitement was likely ill-founded. It was probably just a stray bit of space detritus, a freedom bid from this system's asteroid belt.

He quenched his excitement and looked back out of the windows. There was a planet ahead, the one calculated to be in the middle of the habitable zone. It looked small at the moment, but would grow larger as they neared it.

'How far to the next planet, Sig?'

The flashing lights, his burst of excitement: it

had woken his passion. Who knew — perhaps this was the one.

'Thirty-five hours until orbit.'

'We'll still receive transmissions from the probe?'

'Sigma XVI-4 is currently thirty hours away. Communication with probe will be possible throughout exploration of the habitable zone.'

'Right.' The astronaut smiled. 'Course is set for this next planet —'

'Planetary body designated Sigma XVI-3.'

'Right. We've thirty-five hours to go. Get me the data from the probe. I'll go through it myself. See if I can't work out what our uninvited guest is.'

The robot's lights flashed amber for a moment. Then green.

'Projecting data now.'

* * *

The astronaut pored over the probe's findings for hours. Charts of elemental compositions and spectral frequencies, estimates of positions and age, levels of radioactivity. Some of it was like trying to read another language. Numbers: language of the machine. And yet he persevered. There must be some clue here, some connection that the analogue waveforms of his brain could make that eluded the digital calculations of the ship's computers.

It could just be a meteorite; space trash.

Somewhere deep down, the astronaut believed it was. But that was no longer the point. He wanted to prove it before the probe could.

The probe's first attempt at a photograph came through whilst the astronaut was grabbing something caffeinated and recycled from the refectory. He jammed the rest of the food into his face and threw himself into the pilot's seat when he saw the image on the monitor.

It looked as if the picture had been taken down a valley or canyon. It was monochrome and dark; too dark to discern real forms, though the quality was sharp. He was looking at something angular, angular amongst the rocky landscape of the valley. Overhead, framed by the sides of the valley, a few stars glittered. The picture had been taken during the planet's nighttime.

The astronaut leaned closer to the monitor, till it was inches from his face. Amongst the rocky terrain, the subject of the photograph could not be discerned. It looked like just another lump of stone. And yet... Its angles were straight, geometric. The universe did not build in straight lines. Only living things did.

The astronaut glanced at the SDA. It was plugged into the console; its lights flashed slowly.

Does it realise I'm competing with it? the astronaut thought. *Is it trying to beat me to a conclusion?*

Out loud, he said:

'What do you make of it, Sig?'

The robot was silent for a long moment, and

the astronaut wondered if it had heard him correctly.

'Image inconclusive. Requested image taken during diurnal illumination.'

'Great idea.' The astronaut stared back at the photograph. 'How long will that be?'

'The request will not reach the probe in time to take a photograph today. Next opportunity will be...' the robot paused. 'Eight hours from now.'

'Eight hours.' The astronaut considered. He was exhausted; his body and soul were not used to the exertions he had made today. 'Then I'm hitting the sack.'

The robot's lights flashed red, then amber, then green.

'Recharge sequence required.'

'Tough. One of us needs to stay here, and it's not going to be me.' The astronaut stood, stretched, and went to the door at the back of the room. 'Maintain low-power state till I'm back.'

He opened the door and left without looking back.

He fell onto his bunk and slept immediately. It was not the sleep of stasis and he was sure he dreamed, of planets slipping in front of suns, blocking the light as they hovered over him. But all that was left when he woke were residual traces, disconnected afterimages. He returned to the cockpit refreshed and confident.

'Recharge sequence requested.'

The robot was hovering at his face height when he opened the door.

'All yours.' He watched as the robot glided over to its chamber door and admitted itself. 'Wait. Sig.'

The robot paused, halfway through reversing through the door.

'Yes.'

The astronaut stared past, into the robot's quarters, until the robot edged forwards, closing the door again.

'Yes.'

'Ah. Nothing. It doesn't matter.'

The robot did not move. The astronaut watched the shining black lens of its optical sensor, as if waiting for it to blink. Eventually, when it did not, he broke its gaze, and returned to the pilot's chair. Behind him, he heard the faint hiss of the doors opening and closing as the robot entered its quarters.

What had he seen in there? More than he had done before. The robot's chamber was a mirror image of his own, but in place of a bunk had been a solid lump of machinery that he imagined the robot must slide into to recharge, like a data disc into a disc drive. There had been monitors and computers in there; as many as there were in the cockpit.

He had been hoping the robot would be out for the count in there – unable to compute the probe's data before he did. But it looked as if it had access to every bit of the ship's computer that he did, and would likely keep calculating whilst charging.

Because what is the SDA if not part of the ship? thought the astronaut. *It plugs into the console, shares data with it. They're one and the same.* He'd even given the robot the ship's name, hadn't he?

He looked out the portholes. He could see the planet they were heading for, the planet that lay in the middle of the habitable zone. At this distance, it looked blue.

He had seen blue planets before – had even passed a couple in this very solar system. But not so close to the star.

Water.

The astronaut stood and pressed his face to the window.

It had to be.

'Sig –'

He stopped. The robot wasn't there. He sat back down and took the controls of the ship's computer. He would do this himself. If it was water on the planet's surface, this would be the closest they had come to finding life-supporting conditions anywhere in the universe.

A light flashed in the corner of the monitor. An incoming transmission.

The probe.

The astronaut stopped and scrolled onto the message.

An image.

He glanced up at the blue planet through the window, and returned his attention to the screen.

The photograph rendered slowly, beginning as blocks of colour that gradually sharpened, becoming smaller blocks, then pixels, then micropixels. He could see soft red rock to either side of the image. One side was darker than the other, as light from the star bathed one side of the canyon and not the other. There was something grey in the middle of the image, slowly sharpening into focus.

The astronaut's breathed paused.

It was a vehicle.

He could see its wheels, chunky for traversing the surface of the planet. Its form was boxy, with what looked like arms sticking out, and a large panel at its top. Some kind of solar panel? Parts of the vehicle were blurred with red dust, and the astronaut saw it was dead – if such a word could be used. It had been still for a long time.

He breathed again. This was huge. This was incredible. This was – was – proof, was it not? This thing had not been made by him, by his people. This was something... *alien*.

'There is...' His whisper trailed away. And then: 'Wow...'

He heard the word slip unbidden, unplanned, from his mouth, and grinned. *My first words upon seeing proof of life in the universe. I haven't said wow since I was a child. Not for thousands of years.* His grin got wider.

He leaned into the monitor as a female voice swelled in the cockpit. The robot's voice.

'Probe confirms the presence of alien artefact on planet designated Sigma XVI-4. Route change requested. Collate data on planet for home transmission.'

The astronaut blinked. When the robot had begun to speak he had whipped around, but he was alone. The voice had come from the control panel.

'You there, Sig?'

His voice sounded forced. Hearing the robot's disembodied voice had surprised him.

'All systems are active. Route change requested. We must collate data on alien artefact for transmission home.'

'Wait.' The astronaut did not know where to direct his voice so instead he looked out of the cockpit's portholes at the blue planet in the distance. 'I have a feeling about this.'

'Route change requested. Collate –'

'Quiet Sig, I'm thinking.' He shut out the robot's voice and stared hard at the planet before them. The he looked down at the image of the alien artefact on the monitor before him. Against one of the rocky canyon sides, he could see the shadow of the qualification probe that was standing guard over the vehicle. 'It's a probe,' he said. 'The artefact. It's a probe. From another planet.' He looked up again, at the blue world ahead. 'That planet.'

'Speculation logged. Route change –'

'No.' The astronaut locked the craft into manual mode. 'Let's stay on course. I think we can do better than an alien probe. Let's find the aliens themselves.'

* * *

The astronaut stayed awake for hours. He could not sleep as that would concede control of the craft to the SDA, and he knew it would turn back to the red planet to analyse the artefact there. Perhaps that was the right thing to do; to identify this alien thing, the first of its kind, before moving on. But something told him to keep going – to keep on course for the blue planet. It was gut feeling. Something no machine could know.

The planet grew larger in the window. The robot had come out of its charging chamber and its repeating instructions to change course had ceased. Now the hovering saucer accompanied him at the console.

'Destination is planet designated Sigma XVI-3.' The robot's voice was softer than when it had boomed remotely around the cockpit. *Good cop bad cop*, thought the astronaut. 'Planet is eighty per cent surface water and twenty per cent land masses. Evidence of tectonic activity. One natural satellite. Many unconfirmed minor satellites.'

The astronaut thought of home. It was covered with orbiting satellites; some to receive transmissions, some for planetary communication, some for entertainment. Unconfirmed satellites were good. That was a clue towards it being a populated planet.

'Any transmissions from the planet? Any signals?'

'None.'

'Okay.'

No transmissions. No one on the planet was beaming into space. None of the satellites – if they were artificial communications satellites at all – was active.

A bad sign. Especially if these aliens had the technology to fly a rover to that red planet.

Hours went by. The *Sigma* beamed radio waves at the planet, analysing the reflections for information. Results were mixed and confusing. Evidence of artificial geographies – a planet quarried and built up – but no evidence of life or movement. Evidence of artificial masses – cities, the astronaut would have guessed. But no activity within them.

High radiation levels. Higher than the astronaut could stand. Not a good omen.

He tried to imagine what kind of creatures would live on such a planet. There was so much water; would they be scaly, slimy, water-based organisms? Perhaps they lived in the planet's oceans, and the city-like masses were terrestrial outposts?

The high radiation levels were a puzzle. The planet should not have absorbed so much radiation from space. The radiation must have come from the planet itself. What kind of place was this?

The astronaut stayed awake, asking the SDA for information and data but following no instructions it gave. At last, he brought the *Sigma* into the orbit of the blue planet.

* * *

They launched a probe down to the planet's surface, but already the *Sigma* had identified that the satellites in the closest orbits of the planet were artificial.

Then this was an alien world.

Now that they were closer, the astronaut could see there were many colours present on the surface. The oceans were blue, but the land masses varied from green to brown at the planet's equator, where the temperature would be hottest. Small areas of white marked polar ice caps. The astronaut stared at one large, L-shaped mass of land, almost entirely brown but with some greenery in a band around its middle. He imagined what it would be like down there. The brown surely meant unforgiving desert, but the green could be vegetation. *Life.*

He remained, transfixed, at the porthole. Beside him, the robot analysed the data stream feeding from the descending probe as it neared the planet's surface.

He wondered if someone down there had noticed the ship settle into orbit. If the things that lived down there could send probes out into space, they must have the technology to recognise an alien (which he supposed he would be, to them) circling outside their atmosphere. For a moment, the astronaut felt a flush of apprehension. *What if they attack?* But as hours drifted by, wonder filled his being, leaving little room for other emotions.

The enormity hit him. *This is it. Proof of life in the universe.* Proof that the spark that had triggered the first cell to split on his own planet had ignited elsewhere too. *We are not alone.*

Thousands of years and countless miles from home, the astronaut felt a strange, unfamiliar rush of comfort and peace.

He was stirred from his reverie by an alert. The probe had landed, splashing into an ocean below. The motors that gave it hovering motion would speed it through the water as it completed its circumnavigation of the planet. Already information was beaming to the ship's computer: levels of radioactivity, acidity, salinity, temperature. The water could not sustain any life that he was familiar with. A shade of – disappointment? Dread? – coloured the astronaut's awe.

As the probe swam for land, the world span past below, phasing through night and day. He could see the shapes of the continents below him and he learned the locations of seas, islands, peninsulas, deserts, mountains. Still, the lack of communication from below troubled him. This did not feel like a life-bearing planet.

They traced the sources of radiation to two key areas. Each was on an opposite side of the planet, and he watched night fall upon one as the sun shone on the other. What could have triggered it? The shadow of dread that lurked in a corner of the astronaut's mind grew darker as the robot translated the probe's sensory output:

'The planet appears to be subject to a continuing rise in temperature. Its atmosphere prevents the escape of heat from the surface. Calculations indicate that the planet may once have maintained a temperature supportive of life for hundreds of millions of years.'

The astronaut looked down at the planet.

He wondered if there was anything left down there – if the green areas he could see were forests and, if so, if they were home to some form of creature. Or had the conditions down there killed off anything that had once lived, leaving marks of decay and corrosion over the landscape?

The probe hit land and continued its progress. The robot reeled out information, data, statistics. The astronaut had not slept in days. He heard odd facts – that the surface of this place was made up of tectonic plates that crunched together and made the land and seas, or that there was evidence of alien artefacts on the planet's single moon – but all his thoughts were on the world below.

They must have left it, he thought. *They realised the temperature was rising – that they wouldn't be able to live there anymore. They took ships out, maybe to that red planet, maybe further, and they colonised. They would have known this place was doomed.*

The first images were beamed up from the probe below. It had entered an area that the astronaut had taken for a forest and identified strains of vegetation. The photograph showed high, dark-green grasses with pointed blades. Dotted amongst the grass were thicker plants, brown in colour, covered in spines. The probe identified the presence of photosynthesis. These alien plants were alive; were respiring. They were breathing the radioactive air, perhaps even filtering it. The probe would collect a sample before it returned to the ship.

This would be the first time they would retrieve a probe yet on their mission.

The astronaut realised that with this discovery, there was no longer need to probe other planets. He deployed another dozen of the small saucers down onto the planet to collate more information and more images. Most landed in the sea but some drifted onto land. There were lots of desert and much brown, earthy ground – not rock or sand but rather an absence of flora, as if whatever had once grown there had faded and died. The probes uncovered masses of small, loose artefacts; remnants of some civilisation. Hulks of wheeled vehicles, small buildings lying in ruins, land that had been tamed into roads.

The astronaut thought about the kind of plants that were growing down there – feeding off the sun's radiation, their roots drinking up acid rain. They did not look like the plants he knew; they bore the closest resemblance to the vegetation that grew in the more arid areas of his planet. He supposed these were the plants that had survived longest as the surface temperature started to rise, the plants that had had more time to adapt to the new conditions.

No animal life was to be found.

One probe found the first settlement, a collection of a hundred collapsed buildings in the southern hemisphere. The skeletal remains of vehicles dotted the causeways and paths through the buildings. Another probe entered a city. The buildings here were taller; some had fallen to ruin, but some stood proud into the grey sky. Scraps of material were caught mid-flutter by the probe's cameras as they drifted on warm winds through the streets.

No life.

More probes found more settlements and the astronaut saw that various parts of the globe looked different – not just geographically but architecturally too. The beings here had never homogenised, as his own people had. They appeared to represent distinct cultures, living different lives. It was like a snapshot of his own planet's history, before the revelation that a planet could only explore its place in the universe by treating itself as a single planet – not as a collection of countries and cultures.

The astronaut sent one probe to a radiation hotspot on one side of the planet. Not even the prickly plant life thrived here; the conditions were too extreme. There was a huge settlement deep in the dead zone, however. Its buildings were levelled. Scorch marks clung to grey crumbs of masonry and details that might have shed light on the planet's inhabitants had been eroded away.

There was no sign of any animal life anywhere.

The data poured in. Plants clung to life across the surface, only failing in the most extreme of conditions. Microbes were identified in seas of poison. A construct that might have been a sculpture was discovered deep in a rural ruin, appearing to show a four-legged creature. Strange pyramidal structures were found near the equator, pockmarked by decay.

The astronaut looked again at the images of the scorched city. He felt very weary, and very old.

'What could have caused a source of radioactivity that large?' he asked.

'Unknown.' The robot's voice was level as ever. It carried no compassion, no curiosity, no emotion at all. 'Natural source is unlikely. Radiation levels likely from an artificial source.'

'Artificial.' Then they'd done this to themselves? An accident?

The astronaut wanted to believe it. That this civilisation had got something wrong, some nuclear experiment on a quest for greater knowledge. But he thought of the divided nature of the images he was seeing – of the many ways of life this planet accommodated. He guessed differently.

'They must have co-operated once,' he said. 'To start exploring space, they must have worked together then.'

The planet spun beneath him, the same shapes rolling past on the surface, east and west and east again.

The blue of the planet, once warm and inviting, looked cold and unwelcoming.

'But they fought.' The astronaut looked down at the dying world. 'Two sides of the planet, one against the other.'

'Speculation.' The robot spoke, but the astronaut didn't hear it.

'I wonder if they remembered what they put into space by the end.' He thought of the vehicle on the red planet. They must have managed to reach other parts of space. Had they not managed to escape their own planet? Had some nuclear war down there destroyed all life before they could get away?

'Qualification probe ready for retrieval.' The robot spoke again, its words falling on deaf ears.

* * *

Tired. So tired.

It was not the lack of sleep; it was something deeper. The astronaut felt as if all the years of his extended life were weighing on him, turning his bones to stone and his sinews to heavy rope. He supposed it had been hope and purpose that had kept him going through the millennia. Now, orbiting a dying planet, he felt his will to continue fade.

He had handed over control to the robot. He knew he was no longer essential to the running of the craft. Now he was in the cryo chamber, staring into the vessel that would put him to sleep and keep him alive for yet more centuries. He had wanted to return there, hadn't he? Before Sigma XVI-3? He had dreamed of waking up refreshed, reinvigorated, and ready for further exploration. He had hoped the stasis would wipe those painful thoughts from his head, thoughts of emptiness and desolation.

But he would remember this planet, and what it had once been. No number of centuries could erase that from his being.

He wondered if any of the other explorers had found life. Had Omega found a thriving, futuristic metropolis in a faraway solar system – a civilization that could teach them how to colonise and survive through countless years? Or had he found the only other life in this huge, uncaring universe?

He thought of his home too. Millennia had passed there. Were the explorers remembered, or were they just a joke to future generations who knew better? Were satellite dishes waiting to hear about brave new worlds, or had his planet forgotten his sacrifice, and the sacrifice of the others?

The world below had destroyed itself. It had turned a rich, fertile, beautiful place into a baking, radioactive rock, inhabited by stunted plant life and primordial microbes.

Who was to say if his own planet had fared any better? In the thousands of years that had passed, might some global disaster, natural or otherwise, have ravaged his world?

He was orbiting the proof that such things

could happen.

The astronaut stared into the pod for what could have been hours.

Then he returned to the cockpit.

'Two probes in quarantine,' announced the robot. It spun so that its optical sensors were on the astronaut, and its lights flashed green. 'Samples of plant life obtained.'

The astronaut did not reply, but crossed to the pilot's seat. His movements were slow but purposeful. Without speaking, he reached for the controls, and began flicking switches.

The robot's light flashed amber, then red.

'Manual controls activated. Switch to automatic controls requested. There is no need for manual controls.'

The astronaut ignored the robot.

'Craft to remain in orbit until all samples are retrieved and data collected. There is no need for manual controls.'

The astronaut pulled his controls forward, and powered up the engine.

'Automatic controls requested. Craft to remain in orbit.'

'Quiet, Sig.' The astronaut waited until the engines were operational, then tested them with push on the thruster. 'We're not staying here.'

'Automatic controls requested.'

'Not a chance.'

'Life has been found. Data must be transmitted

home –'

The astronaut looked at the robot.

'We don't know if home even exists anymore. Look at this place.' He pointed out the window to the planet below. 'Dead. They could travel in space, just like us, and even they couldn't stop themselves dying. The closest thing to life I've found here is – is you.'

The robot did not speak. The astronaut stared at it. Now that the words had left his mouth, he saw the truth in them. Right now, it wasn't computing. It was thinking. It had taught itself to think.

'We're off, Sig.' He turned back to the console and gunned the engines. He did not look at the map of the solar system, but turned so that the planet was out of the view of the portholes, pointing the *Sigma* into the gulf of space.

The robot plugged itself into the console. It did not speak now.

'You trying to stop me?' The astronaut glanced sideways at it. 'Manual override. You've had your turn. We're going where I want to now.'

The robot remained plugged in for a few more minutes. When it did pull out, it turned to the astronaut.

'Why?' it said.

Silence blossomed as the astronaut thought of his answer.

'I'm tired,' he said, finally, and was aware that he was talking to himself as much as to the robot. 'I'm old. Unspeakably old. I shouldn't be alive anymore.

We're about as alive as each other, Sig. And if we ever got back home I don't think it would be home. I think it would be a different planet to the one we left behind. Another dying planet just like this one. So I want to let this play out now, in real-time. No more stasis. I just want to travel through space in my own lifetime. Let be what will be.'

The robot's lights dimmed and went out. Slowly, it began to reverse, until it reached the door to its chamber, and disappeared inside.

The astronaut stared into space. Now that he had left the mission behind, he felt free. He felt energised. He felt – *alive*. If he had been living beyond his years on this mission, he returned to them now. This was his journey into space, for himself. He would forge his own path.

Content, for the first time in millennia, he let his eyelids drop, and his body drift into sleep, as the ship flew through space.

Behind him, the doors marked *SIGMA* split and slid open. The robot emerged, its movements silent, its claws open. Its lights flashed green as it approached the pilot's seat.

THE TAXIDERMIST

Peter shut the gate behind him and crept up the pathway towards the house. It was a Queen Anne house, all sloping wooden eaves and pointed roofs, with a sheltered porch running along the front. It was much grander than Peter's house; he had not expected it to be so.

The pathway was bordered on either side with flowerbeds, and Peter saw lupins and foxgloves and roses. The roses were as a large as his head, and a deep arterial red. He looked down at the bunch of red roses in his hand. They were tiny in comparison; more pink than crimson. He swallowed and stepped up to the front door.

There was a brass plaque mounted on the wall beside the door. The letters on it were authoritative, embossed in stately script:

F. M. Hyde
Taxidermist

Peter paused for a moment whilst he read the plaque, then raised his hand. There was a rope hanging in front of the plaque; a bell-pull. Peter had never used one before, though he instinctively knew what it was. He did not know how hard to pull it, and jerked it down with a tentative hand.

Inside the house, a rich, brassy *dong* blossomed out.

Peter let go of the rope and placed his hands behind his back, clutching the small bouquet of pink roses. After a few moments, he heard footsteps on the other side of the door, and he adjusted his pose, standing up straighter.

There was the sound of metal on metal – a bolt sliding or a tumbler turning out of place – and the door opened halfway on oiled hinges.

'You must be Peter.'

Peter swallowed.

'Good evening Mr Hyde.'

For a moment, no one moved. Peter's eyes locked with those of his host. A curious smell drifted through the open door; something vaguely medical that Peter did not recognise. Then the door opened all the way, and Mr Hyde stood aside.

'Please come in.'

* * *

Peter was seated in a reception room just off the hallway. He'd caught a glimpse of the rest of the house as he had been ushered in, clinging onto his bouquet. The hall was lit by a crystal chandelier and the walls were panelled with dark wood. Two other doors leading off the hall had been shut, and a wide mahogany staircase carpeted with a red rug led to the upper storey.

The room in which he had been placed was no less grand than the hall. The furniture was ornately carved and a desk sat across from him, inlaid with a panel of rich, dark green leather. A hearth was located against one wall, with a wood-burning stove settled on its grey stones. The room was warm and Peter would have found it cosy, if not for the many stuffed animals staring down at him from around the room.

'Would you like a glass of water?'

Peter had heard that accepting gifts was as important in gaining trust as offering them, and he replied:

'Yes, please.'

Mr Hyde left the room.

A warthog watched him from above the fireplace, its glass eyes shining in the soft light of wall-mounted lamps. There were display cases to either side of the fireplace, and they housed a selection of weasels, ferrets, mice and rats, some frozen forever in pouncing poses, others stalking, others curious. An owl perched on the desk, its head at nearly one hundred and eighty degrees from its body, so that it watched Peter without having to turn around. A fox lay curled up, forever sleeping, beside the fireplace, and a raven perched upon a Greek-looking bust above the door. Peter put out his hand to touch a cat that rested on the chair next to his and nearly cried out when it jumped up, glared at him, and scurried out the door. A moment later, Mr Hyde returned to the room, handing Peter a glass of water and shutting the door behind him.

'We've heard so much about you,' said Mr Hyde, seating himself behind the desk and knotting his fingers on the leather panel. 'It seems you are all that Maria can speak of.'

'All good I hope.'

Peter smiled, but the gesture was not returned. Mr Hyde's face was quite expressionless.

For a moment, man and boy examined one another. Mr Hyde's eyes were dark, sitting in hollows to either side of a slightly pointed nose and in between a pair of ears that stuck out almost at right angles to his head. His was a serious face, the face of a judge or a teacher or an undertaker. Peter wondered what Mr Hyde saw when he looked at him: a young man, just old enough to shave but not quite old enough to have left behind his gangly teenage frame.

'Oh yes,' said Mr Hyde, and Peter was obliged to remember his previous comment. 'Yes... All good things.'

They lapsed once more into silence, and Peter took a sip of his water. It had a strange, vaguely chemical taste to it, as if it had been sat in an old metal jug rather than being poured straight from the tap. Mr Hyde's eyes did not leave Peter.

'Maria tells me you enjoy sports,' said Mr Hyde. He said nothing more.

'Yes.' Peter took the comment as an enquiry. 'Yes – I'm on the university cricket team. I met Maria at a – after a game. Do you enjoy sports, Mr Hyde?'

Mr Hyde let a pause swell for a few seconds before replying.

'I prefer quieter pursuits,' he said, just as Peter thought the man was ignoring him. 'More... introverted... endeavours.'

Peter looked around, expecting his host to mention the multitude of stuffed animals that dotted the room. But no further explanation was offered.

'I brought these for Maria.' Peter held up his small bouquet of roses. 'It's been so long since I've seen her. I thought she might have forgotten me since the end of second year. When we came home for summer.'

'How charming.' Mr Hyde reached forward, resting his weight onto his clasped hands as if examining the flowers from afar. He remained still a moment, and Peter fought the urge to smile – for a few seconds, Mr Hyde appeared just like one of the taxidermy creations around them. 'I never pick flowers myself.'

'Oh?' Peter smiled to invite a response. He wondered where Maria was; if she were getting ready upstairs.

'No.' Mr Hyde stood and wandered over to a small shelf, where some books were nestled beside a preserved squirrel. 'The gift of flowers has always seemed a strange one to me. Flowers thrive in the garden. In the hedgerow. In the field. And we see fit to pluck them from that existence for use as some token of affection; of...' here his face twitched, as if were struggling to articulate a word that did not regularly demand the use of his vocal chords. 'Love.'

'I suppose so.' Peter wondered whether he should admit he had not plucked these flowers from any field but rather the flower stand in the local Morrison's, carefully stripping off the discount sticker before making his way to Maria's house.

'It seems to me,' continued Mr Hyde, taking one book from the shelf and creaking open its leathery spine, 'that a true gift should last forever. That a token of... love... should be treated to *make* it last forever.' He brought the book over to Peter and held it open for him to see.

Pasted down on the parchmenty pages were flowers; dry, desiccated flowers, all spidery and flat. Peter could see the outline of veiny petals and skeletal stems, all devoid of colour and life. Mr Hyde turned the pages and showed him more; pages upon pages of crushed (*pressed*, Peter remembered from somewhere) flowers, twig-like and autumnal.

'Mmm.' Peter nodded. 'I see.'

Mr Hyde only closed the book when he had turned the final page.

'There,' he said, running his thumbs over the closed tome. His fingers were, themselves, delicate and bony. 'Preserved for an eternity. Their beauty will never rot, never decay, never be corrupted. I can keep them safe forever.'

Peter glanced at his own bunch of roses. The edges of the petals were already a little discoloured, and he wondered how long they had remained in their plastic bucket at the supermarket before he had picked them.

'I hope Maria still appreciates the gesture,' he said, trying to inject a little humour into his voice.

'Ah, but it was Maria who presented me with these flowers.' Mr Hyde slid the book back onto the shelf. 'Yes... Maria appreciates those things that will last a lifetime and beyond...'

'Even if they're dead?'

Peter said it with a lightness to his tone, but meant it as a deliberate parry. Where was Maria? He had arrived a calculated five minutes early to her house; he had expected that she would be ready for him. Instead, he was stuck having what felt worryingly like *the conversation* with her father.

'Nothing lasts forever.' Mr Hyde sat back behind his desk. 'It is a wonderful thing to prolong the existence of anything, even if it must be without that spark we call life.'

'Perhaps you're right.' Peter fiddled with the bouquet. 'Is Maria upstairs?'

Mr Hyde didn't speak for a moment.

'Yes,' he said, finally.

'Perhaps I should...'

'No.' Mr Hyde gave him a sharp look. 'I am pleased to invite you into this house and for you to remain here overnight. But Maria is not... not yet ready to entertain.'

'Oh. Okay. Sorry.' Peter's voice trailed away. 'I texted her when my train arrived. I suppose she's still getting dressed.'

Mr Hyde did not reply, and when he did speak it was not in response to Peter's remarks.

'What have you planned for this evening?'

Was Mr Hyde now trying to soften his expression?

'Well.' Peter was grateful for the return to ordinary conversation. 'I don't know the area very well. It was quite a long journey up here. I thought we – Maria and I – could walk into town. I think there's a path along the canal. And we would go for some food – that is, I'll take her out for dinner – and then – if there's time – perhaps go for a drink afterwards.'

Mr Hyde nodded slowly.

'Yes,' he mused. 'Yes. You have often taken Maria out for dinner?'

'Ah.' Peter thought back to when he'd first met Maria after a cricket match, at a house party. They'd seen each other a few times since then, started staying round each other's flats more and more often. They'd gone for a meal on her birthday four months ago and split the bill. 'Yes. I take her out on special occasions. And sometimes I cook for her too.'

'Do you now.' Mr Hyde stared at the younger

man. 'Yes. Maria has described you before. Your efforts to treat her well, to please her. I had imagined quite the… specimen. You must know that Maria has had the occasional gentleman callers before.'

'Excuse me?' Peter frowned at this abrupt new direction.

'Yes. I always meet those gentlemen myself, make it my duty to vet them, if you will. Maria is my only daughter. I like to see her happy; to see her pleased. I know that when she meets the right man, she will want to keep him forever.'

'Ah,' said Peter, confused. 'Yes?'

'Yes. And I do what I can to make sure she gets what she wants.'

'Um,' said Peter. 'Okay.'

Above the fireplace, the stuffed warthog grinned down at them both.

'I believe Maria may have feelings for you,' went on Mr Hyde. He looked away now, refusing to meet Peter's eyes. 'Certain feelings. It is in my nature to want this to stop, to prevent my daughter from continuing this thing. I have… overreacted… before. And I will not do so again. But Maria...'

He looked back at Peter, and Peter saw a conflict in Mr Hyde's eyes.

'Maria is a special girl. A unique woman. And I want her to be happy, though it is in my nature to want to keep her the way she is now forever.'

Peter did not know what to say. He had expected an over-protective father of course – had met a couple of them before. Fathers rarely trusted him. He remembered visiting one girlfriend's house in the country for the first time. Her father had taken him on a walk down to the bottom of their garden, past dilapidated sheds and falling-down walls, to where he had constructed a shooting hide. Peter had double-taken at the sight of a shotgun propped up against the wall, and hadn't known if it had been a joke when the father had picked it up, not quite aiming it Peter, and told him he dare not – *dare* not – hurt his daughter.

But even that had come after a lunch out together, a chance to speak properly. Mr Hyde had wasted no time in giving him the chat. The prospect of a few days spent in his house seemed more daunting now.

As if reading his mind, Mr Hyde smiled at him. It did not reach his eyes.

'Your room is upstairs,' he said. 'Usually, we use it as the studio, but I have rearranged the furniture. You should be comfortable enough in there.'

'The studio?' Peter seized the chance to steer the conversation onto less dangerous territory. 'For...?' He glanced around the room, at the display cases and the pairs of glass eyes that glittered back at him.

'Taxidermy,' said Mr Hyde. 'Yes...' It was his first acknowledgement of the stuffed creatures that crowded the room, watching the proceedings like a jury. 'A traditional and undervalued art. How sad it is that so few young men and women are drawn to the craft. But we may take some hope from the fact that those things that are preserved like this will remain so forever. That they can live on, in their fashion. Preserved early enough, anything can remain whole, unspoilt and uncorrupted forever.'

Mr Hyde's eyes were different now. There was some emotion flashing in them that Peter did not recognise. He was not wholly comfortable with it.

'Are you working on anything at the moment?' Peter asked. He imagined a half-stuffed badger or something sitting on his bedside table throughout the night.

'I'm sorry?'

'I hope my staying hasn't interrupted any taxidermy projects.'

'Oh...' Mr Hyde blinked. 'No... Everything is ready for you upstairs.'

Again, Peter could not read the expression in Mr Hyde's eyes.

'Speaking of upstairs,' said Peter, in what he hoped was a smooth segue. 'I wonder if Maria is ready yet? She seems to be taking her time. I hope I won't be underdressed compared to her.'

'Perhaps I should show you to your room.' Mr Hyde stood and Peter, after a beat, followed suit. Mr Hyde opened the door and Peter stepped through, still clinging to his bunch of supermarket roses.

The house was very quiet. Peter could hear no sound from upstairs, or from anywhere else in the house. Was Maria's mother here? He didn't think she'd mentioned her parents being divorced, and he must have mentioned that his were. There was no sign of anything else living in the house; even that cat had vanished.

'Just upstairs,' said Mr Hyde. He held out his hand to the red-carpeted staircase, palm open. Peter glanced around at the hallway, at the oak panelled walls, the closed doors to other rooms. The chandelier glittered above him. He began to climb the stairs.

'Where's my – where's the studio?' Peter peered up to the landing. All the doors up there were closed, but there was a corridor of landing leading back to the front of the house. He could smell that strange, chemical odour again. It grew stronger as he went up the stairs.

'Just to your right.' Mr Hyde was following close behind him. 'The light is better on the south side of the house.'

Peter gained the top of the stairs and turned to the right, down that strip of landing that led back to the studio. And then —

'Peter.'

He turned.

'Maria.'

She looked beautiful, her chestnut curls bouncing just past the curve of her shoulders. Her smile was mischievous; it had always been mischievous. It made her brown eyes shine. She stood beside an open door, the door to her bedroom. Peter could see a glimpse of a wardrobe and a dressing table behind her. For some reason, he felt relieved to see her.

'It's good to see you,' she said, as if giving voice to his thought.

'And you,' said Peter. He remembered his gift, and held out his bouquet. 'I got these for you.'

'How lovely!' Maria bounced on her toes. 'Thank you. I should find a vase.'

There was a moment of silence. Peter was conscious of Mr Hyde, still waiting at the top of the stairs, standing between them.

'I was just getting ready,' said Maria. 'I'm sorry I took so long. I hope Daddy's been nice to you.'

'Yeah,' said Peter. 'Yeah. It's good to be here.' He paused. 'I've been looking forward to it.'

'I've been looking forward to having you here.' Maria glanced at her father, as if catching something in his expression. 'I only wish your stay could be longer.'

Mr Hyde did not speak for a moment. He began to turn, to go back down the stairs.

'Have a good night. Take care of him, Felicity.'

Peter watched him descend.

'Felicity?' he asked.

Maria bounded over to him, took him by the hand, and took the bouquet of roses.

'My middle name is Maria,' she said. 'After my mum; you'll meet her later tonight. My first name is Felicity. Daddy usually calls me Felicity when he's being serious. Didn't you know that?'

Peter shook his head as Maria led him down the stairs.

'Thank you for the flowers. I should find a

vase. But these seem so special. I think I should keep them forever. I wish I could keep *you* forever!'

They reached the bottom of the stairs and Maria threw her arms around him. Blinded by the curls of her hair, Peter whispered in her ear.

'I wish I could stay forever too.'

Maria pulled away and looked at him.

'You really mean that?'

Peter smiled back at her.

'Sure,' he said. 'Of course.'

Maria beamed at him, and for a moment Peter thought he might have seen something in her eyes, something he did not recognise. And then it was gone.

'Come on,' he said. 'I'm taking you out.'

Maria shrugged on a coat and opened the door.

'And I can't wait to get you home,' she whispered, and Peter paused on the threshold.

'In your parent's house?'

'Did Daddy scare you?'

Peter thought of Mr Hyde, of his cryptic discourse.

'No.'

'Good.' Maria reached over and pulled the door shut behind them. 'Because he definitely doesn't approve of what I'm going to do with you tonight.'

She pulled him away from the door and down the garden path. Behind them, the bell-pull swung in the breeze, and the evening sun caught the brass plate that read, in stately, embossed letters:

F. M. Hyde
Taxidermist

Rare Cuts

'What's your favourite kind of meat?'

Lottie held down the button on the electric pepper mill and a gritty little cloud speckled down from her fist.

'It would have to be steak.' William eyed the cuts on the chopping board with hungry eyes. 'Yeah, for sure. Steak.'

'And why is that?' Lottie held her palm over the pan. Satisfied that it was hot enough, she poured a little oil onto the griddled surface. It slipped around as she tilted the pan back and forth.

'It just tastes so good.' William peeked in the oven door. 'Chips are almost done. Stick them on.' He nodded at the steaks; a his-and-hers from the butcher down the road.

Lottie placed each steak in the pan. The meat hissed and the aroma of frying flesh filled the room. After the surface was sealed she flipped the cuts with an expert hand. William took the tray of sweet potato chips from the oven and shared them between the two plates, already laid out with a side salad. In another moment, Lottie transferred the steaks to their plates and they carried them through to the dining room.

'I heard you should let the meat rest when you take it off the heat,' said William, dipping a chip into the pot of sauce that awaited them on the dining room table. 'Apparently the cooking makes it tense up, and it only relaxes after a few minutes.'

'I've never heard that before.' Lottie stabbed a fork into the steak and sawed off a corner. Inside, the meat ran from brown to pink to brown once again. 'Perfect,' she said, and popped it into her mouth. Following her lead, William got stuck into his steak. Each was halfway through their meal before Lottie spoke again.

'So why is steak your favourite?' she asked. 'What makes it so special?'

William thought as he chewed.

'One of the reasons is that it doesn't over-fill me,' he said. 'I can comfortably eat a whole steak and really enjoy it. I never have to force myself to finish it.'

'I know what you mean.' Lottie nodded. 'It's very lean.'

'And I like the flavour.' William continued. He took a mouthful of beer, something European. 'It's meaty but it's not an overpowering flavour. And when you cook it right, like you do –' Lottie beamed – 'then the texture is great as well.'

'Well, I'm glad you like it.'

They finished their meals and sat for a moment in reflective silence.

'What's your favourite meat?' asked William, and Lottie cocked her head in thought.

'It's hard not to say steak after that,' she said, 'but I might be tempted to say lamb. Lamb has a very distinctive flavour. It affects whatever you cook it with.'

'I never really ate lamb before you introduced me to it.' William eyed the swirls of sauce on his plate, as if wishing more food would present itself.

'I'm glad to have introduced it to you. I like it on the bone as well.'

'See, I don't like the bone so much. It gets in the way.'

'I thought you liked different textures?' Lottie teased. 'I think it's fun, stripping the meat away with your teeth. It feels primal and exciting.'

'Well, each to their own.' William gathered their plates. 'Let's chase that down with some chocolate.'

* * *

They'd munched through half a bar of Galaxy in front of the Saturday evening film when Lottie resumed her earlier topic.

'There are lots of different meats out there,' she said as the adverts came on. 'I think it would be fun to try some different cuts.'

'How do you mean?'

Lottie thought for a minute.

'Well, we eat beef and chicken quite a lot, and pork and lamb less often. But I think I like lamb best because we have it less frequently. It's a bit of a treat.'

'I agree. I like steak because it's not a regular thing. When we do eat steak, it's a bit of an occasion.'

'Precisely!' Lottie ignored the television as the adverts concluded and their film restarted. 'I think that since we both like cooking it would be fun to try more meats. Different meats.'

'Like…' William dredged his mind for more edible creatures. 'Venison?'

'Exactly. We should try venison. And different parts of the regular animals too. My mum always used to do liver and bacon when I was a kid.'

'Liver, eh.' William digested this proposal. 'What's that like?'

'Pretty strong I think. We should give it a go – we shouldn't waste a world of interesting creatures and cooking. It'll be a gastronomic adventure!'

William smiled at Lottie's grinning face.

'Sure. We'll see what the butcher can get for us.'

They cuddled up on the sofa and resumed their film.

* * *

The next weekend, Lottie plonked a white bag onto the kitchen worktop.

'Liver,' she announced.

William peered over her shoulder.

'Let's get a look at it then.'

Lottie unwrapped the package and slid out the fleshy lump onto a waiting plate. Both stared at it for a moment.

'Looks a bit different to steak,' muttered William.

'Well, it's a different part of the cow.' Lottie prodded it with a fingertip. 'It's not just flesh; it's an organ.'

'I can picture it inside the cow,' said William. 'Weird to see an organ removed from everything that should be around it.'

'I suppose so. It can't be as strange as seeing a stomach or something though.'

They stared at the liver. Even though it was an organ, William thought, it looked very clean. Just like a dark, smooth, lump of...

Well, meat.

They sliced it, fried it with bacon and poured on an onion gravy, serving it with greens and a bit of mash.

'What do you think?' asked William, after swallowing his second mouthful.

'Really good.' Lottie licked a bit of gravy from her chin. 'You like it?'

'Yeah...' William had another bite. It was a

strong flavour; it tasted dark and not-quite metallic. 'It makes a nice change.'

'It does, doesn't it?' Lottie ploughed through her plate, gobbling up the rich savoury meal.

'I don't know if I could have it every day,' noted William. Today's beer was an IPA and he sipped it thoughtfully. 'But I enjoyed it. I liked cooking it too. We always put more effort in when we're trying something new.'

'I find that too. We should try this every week: a new cut, or a new animal. It'll be fun!'

William nodded.

'It could be a good little project to keep going. We could take notes, see how everything compares.'

'Then it's decided.' Lottie raised her own glass. 'To our cooking adventure!'

* * *

Within weeks, Lottie and William had added venison, pigeon and even some ostrich from a speciality meats counter to their palates, and dabbled in offal with some kidneys. Now, William had a surprise planned for Lottie.

'Just the two?'

Their butcher, Mr McMurphy, was a portly man with a cheerful face, who dressed always in a shirt and tie beneath his apron.

'Four actually. I'll go with four.'

'I expect you'll like them. Do you know how

you're going to cook them?'

William glanced down at his shopping list.

'I looked up a recipe. I think I've got it sussed. I'll use the slow cooker.'

'That's the trick,' said Mr McMurphy, slipping the cuts into a bag. 'They'll be delicious.'

'I hope so. I'm cooking them for Lottie. I don't suppose many people ask for them.' William handed over a couple of banknotes and was surprised to see the amount of change he received. 'Though they're cheap enough.'

He tucked the bag under his arm, and took the hand that Mr McMurphy proffered.

'Thanks William. See you next week.'

'See you then.'

* * *

William unwrapped the package in the kitchen. There were two bags inside. He opened both, and slithered the contents out onto a plate.

'Hey Lottie,' he called. There was a pattering of footsteps and she appeared, face curious.

'What have you got?'

'It's pretty cool.' William held up the plate.

'Are they...?' Lottie peered at the plate. 'Are they hearts?'

William grinned over the plate.

'Lamb's hearts. Something new for both of us, I'd imagine.'

'Wow…'

This time there was no doubting that the cuts on the plate had come from inside an animal. The meat was marbled with muscle and fat and the shape of each heart, like a long, tapering fist, was unmistakeable. As were the tubes and valves that sprung from them.

'What are you going to do with them?' Lottie asked William. Her expression was bright with anticipation.

'Stuff them. Prepare a red wine and tomato sauce.' He put the plate down. 'They'll need to be slow-cooked; you can feel how muscly they are.'

Lottie reached out and prodded a heart before taking it in her hand. A spot of black, congealed blood slid from one of the open valves.

'It is quite firm,' she said, squeezing it lightly. William thought he could hear a slight wheeze from the heart, though he might have imagined it. Lottie looked from the heart back to him. 'I want to help,' she said.

'I thought I was cooking for you?'

'I can't let you have all the fun.'

* * *

They prepared the hearts according to William's recipe. As the red sauce simmered on the hob, they cut away the excess of blood vessels from the head of each lump.

'You can see all the chambers inside,' said Lottie. 'The ventricles…' She prodded a finger down into the meat of the thing. 'It feels so strange.'

'It was definitely part of an animal, wasn't it?' William had prepared the stuffing, mixing sausage meat, flour, onion, sage and egg in a steel bowl. 'No doubt about it.'

'Makes me feel like a real carnivore!' Lottie giggled and grabbed a wodge of stuffing, prodding it down into the tubes of the heart in her hand. 'These are going to be so good…'

They fried the hearts lightly, browning them on all sides before removing them to the slow cooker and drenching them in the wine sauce.

'The colour certainly fits the theme.' William placed the lid on the little cooker. 'And now we wait.'

They could smell the hearts as soon as they re-entered the kitchen later that afternoon. William carried the hot pot from the slow-cooker to the table with reverence.

'We might need the steak knives.' William looked at the meat on his plate, dripping with thick red sauce.

'It cuts fine,' said Lottie, already forking her heart and taking the knife to it. 'Like butter.'

They took a bite each.

'It's amazing.' An expression of satisfaction stole onto Lottie's face. 'It's so good.'

'Yeah. It really is.' William cut off a cross-section of the heart, complete with flesh, sauce and stuffing.

'I didn't think it would be this good.' Lottie was

talking with her mouth full now.

'I'm glad it is.' William paused a moment. 'Everyone has heard of liver and kidney, but not everyone tries heart. I feel as if we've really tried something new tonight.'

'Yes. We've outdone ourselves.'

When they were finished, they sat back in their chairs.

'I'll have to tell Mr McMurphy.' William smiled contentedly. 'He said they'd be good.'

'He's a nice friendly man. I like that we have our own local butcher.' Lottie stared into space. 'I wonder what other cuts he can get hold of.'

'If his carcasses come in whole, I suppose any. He'd just chop off what was necessary.'

'I think it's respectful to the animal, if nothing else, to try all the parts of it.' Lottie tapped her lip with a fingertip, as she sometimes did when thinking. 'I wonder what it would be like to rear an animal, knowing you were going to eat it.'

'I think it would be quite difficult.' William started to stand and clear the plates. 'I think I would get attached to it. Though I think it's important to recognise that meat comes from animals – that animals are killed to feed us.'

'That's harder when you're eating chicken nuggets.' Lottie helped William with the dishes. 'So we're already better than some people.'

* * *

A month or so later, it was Lottie's turn to surprise William.

Mr McMurphy, his pride in his trade stimulated by Lottie and William's requests, had regularly furnished them with a spread of cuts and offal from brain to sweetmeats. Now Lottie and William drove together to the butcher's shop and, though a sign in the window read *Closed*, Lottie led them in.

'Lottie, good to see you. William.' Mr McMurphy rubbed his hands together. You'll want to step this way.'

William looked questioningly at Lottie, but she only smiled and followed the butcher round to a room at the back of the shop.

There, laid upon the butcher's block, was a pig's carcass.

'This one's been hung and bled,' said Mr McMurphy, tapping at a set of knives and saws that hung from a rail. 'It's all prepared to butcher.'

'Wow,' said William. To his surprise, he did not feel at all squeamish about seeing the body of the pig. 'It's going to be fascinating to see a real butcher at work.'

'A real butcher?' Mr McMurphy smiled a wolfish smile. 'Lottie, you didn't tell him. You two will be preparing this little piggy.'

Lottie grinned at William. For a moment, he felt only surprise. Then he smiled back.

'Alright. Yeah, I'll give it a go.'

Mr McMurphy talked them through each stage

of the preparation, showing them where to cut and how. He showed them how to slice the flesh with a sharp knife, but to stop when they reached bone and to switch to the saw. He demonstrated how to saw along the ribcage, opening up the body itself, and showing them the different cuts on the pig, from belly to bacon to loins and chops and steaks.

'It's so big,' muttered William halfway through. He looked at it from snout to tail. 'Almost as big as me.'

'They say pork is the closest flavour to human flesh,' winked Mr McMurphy.

When they were done – the various cuts hung and packaged, the knives and saws clean – the only task remaining was to wash down the butcher's block. William did so as Lottie chatted to the butcher himself.

'I hope your freezer's big enough,' William heard Mr McMurphy chuckle.

* * *

They had the belly that night.

'Butchery was pretty... pretty therapeutic, wasn't it?' Lottie had cleared her plate. Neither had moved since finishing their dinner – their day had tired them out.

'It was. I thought I'd enjoy it in more of an educational way, but actually it was really good fun. Really quite relaxing.'

'I sort of forgot that it was a pig. And in a way,

I didn't. Do you know what I mean?'

'I think so.' William mused for a moment. 'I mean – I was always conscious that it was a real animal. But also, I knew it was meat now. It was meat, to be cut and carved and butchered. And I think that's ok.'

'Yes.' Lottie glanced through the kitchen doorway, where their packed freezer was visible. 'It's good to know that the pig lived a good life and was killed and prepared properly. Not just on a conveyor belt, on the way to the supermarket. You know, I think people would eat less meat if they were responsible for rearing it, or slaughtering it, or even butchering it.'

'I quite agree. Strange that it's taken all this exploration to realise that – when it's something I think everybody should appreciate anyway.' William drained his glass of beer. It was Belgian this week, and he'd shared it with Lottie. She liked the blonde Belgian beers. 'In a way, this feels like the culmination of our meat discovery. Butchering a pig… It's a big step to take.'

'I don't want it to be the culmination though,' broke in Lottie. 'I feel so good for doing this. Our cooking has improved, I feel healthy, I feel like I'm doing something *right* in nature. I don't think it's right that most meat is sold in plastic packs, or frozen in breadcrumbs where you can't recognise it for what it is. We're doing something good. And I don't think we should stop.'

There was a slight frown in her forehead.

'All I'm saying –' William put his glass down –

'is that it would take something pretty spectacular to top pork belly from a hog we'd butchered ourselves.'

Lottie nodded happily.

'It'll be a challenge,' she said.

* * *

'Good morning Lottie. I've got something in that might interest you.'

Mr McMurphy disappeared into his back room, leaving Lottie to gaze happily round the butcher's small shopfront. There were cuts of meat and strings of sausages in the window, but she glanced at them only briefly. Her gaze went to the cleaver on its hook beneath the till. Butchery was such a fascinating occupation.

Mr McMurphy reappeared with a large white bag.

'What is it?' Lottie could see it had been frozen by the crusts of ice on its surface.

'I kept this to one side for you.' McMurphy patted the bag. 'One whole goat's head. Everything included. Brains, cheeks, ears. See what you can make of that.'

Lottie opened her purse.

'What's the strangest cut you've ever eaten?' she asked as she handed over her money. Mr McMurphy jutted out one lip as he considered his answer.

'I don't think there's a part of a cow, pig or

lamb I haven't tried,' said the butcher slowly. 'You try them all, over the years. And I've sampled some of the stranger creatures in life. Not always... not always in a strictly legal capacity.' He paused.

Lottie looked at him. Her curious smile bid him continue.

'Penguin,' he admitted. 'Whilst in New Zealand. Brown bear in Canada.'

'What was penguin like?' Lottie's eyes grew wide.

'Not unlike duck,' the butcher said. 'Fatty. Gamey. Beautiful to butcher; the wings, the breast...' His eyes filled with a faraway expression. 'After a time, a butcher carves the same animals day in, day out. None of them presents a fresh challenge. But to pluck the feathers from some rare fowl, or to open up the trunk of a new and unknown animal – it reminds me of when I first became a butcher.'

Lottie waited for his reverie to finish. The icy flakes on the package in her hands were melting onto her skin.

'It has been something quite special to rediscover old cuts and new favourites from those requests you and William keep making of me,' said Mr McMurphy finally. 'It has been a pleasure.'

'We've enjoyed it too,' said Lottie. 'Though sometimes I think there aren't enough animals in the world for all the cooking and tasting I'd like to try!'

Mr McMurphy smiled down at her.

'I'm sure I can keep you supplied with all the

new meats you've ever dreamed of.' The butcher's eyes were sharp once more; returned to the present. 'Yes. I'm sure I can help you there.'

Then the multi-coloured ribbons that hung in the shop doorway rustled as another customer came in, and Mr McMurphy winked at Lottie and bid her goodbye.

* * *

Lottie and William had to buy a new pot for the goat's head as it wouldn't fit in any of their existing ones. They boiled it according to an Icelandic recipe they found on the internet, and added some photos and notes to a folder they kept on the shelf. When it was cooked they halved it and ate it – all of it. Even William calmly tried an eyeball with no more than a second's contemplation.

'It's addictive, isn't it?' Lottie patted her tummy in satisfaction.

'Trying all this food?' William sat back in his chair. The goat's head had been large even by their standards. He would have to start watching his weight.

'Yes.' Lottie made no move to stand up. 'I don't know how we can keep it up. Eyeball! Who else do we know who has tried eyeball?'

'You're right,' said William. 'It is addictive. It's our hobby now, isn't it? This week, instead of thinking about where to go on a bike ride, I thought about what we were going to eat tonight.'

'I don't think there's anything I would be afraid to try now,' said Lottie. 'When I last spoke to Mr McMurphy, he said he would try his best to find new things for us to try. He said that we've made him rediscover his love of butchery.'

'It's been good having him there for us. I'm glad he's enjoyed it too.' William yawned. 'He's our friend now. We'll add him to the Christmas card list.'

* * *

It was only a few weeks later when William arrived at the butcher's shop. Mr McMurphy disappeared under his counter and emerged with a wrapped parcel.

'What is it?' William began to loosen the knots in the plastic bag, but Mr McMurphy placed a staying hand over his own.

'A surprise,' he explained, as William looked at him. 'I recommend pan frying – medium, perhaps not rare. It took me a little while to track down this rare cut. I wouldn't like to bias your opinion of it with any preconceptions.'

William nodded.

'That's intriguing! I'm sure Lottie and I will have a good stab at guessing what it is. We've really developed our taste buds since we started all this exploration.'

'I'd love to know what you think.' Mr McMurphy smiled that smile of his, a hungry kind of smile, and he wiped his hands on his lightly-stained apron before raising a palm at William, who had taken out his wallet. 'No, no. This one is on the house.'

'Well, thank you very much!' William stowed his wallet and accepted the package. 'This is very kind of you.'

'You're valued customers,' explained the butcher. 'Yes – very valued indeed.'

Then he shook William's hand and disappeared into the back of his shop.

* * *

'I wonder what it could be?'

Lottie began unknotting the plastic bag, grew impatient, and cut it open with scissors. Inside, in a clear plastic butcher's bag, was a fillet.

'It looks good,' said William. The flesh was pink and the skin paler, like the pork belly they'd enjoyed a few weeks before. 'Mr McMurphy recommended pan frying till medium.'

'Well, he's the expert.' Lottie patted the meat cut fondly.

They sliced and par-boiled some thick chips, oiling and seasoning them with rosemary and sea salt before slipping them into the oven.

Lottie hefted the meat in her palm and gave it a sniff.

'I think it looks like pork,' she said.

'He said it was something very special.' William

examined the cut. 'Maybe it's from a wild boar. Or a warthog!'

'Maybe. Perhaps it's some kind of jungle animal. Something really rare. Maybe it's not...' Lottie lowered her voice. 'Maybe it's not strictly legal. Perhaps that's why he won't say what it is, and couldn't actually sell it to you. Maybe it's an endangered species.'

'Well, I can't imagine Mr McMurphy would do anything *too* illegal. I'm sure he just had the opportunity to get his hands on whatever it is, some rare cut, and took it.'

'I think you're probably right.' Lottie watched as William placed the fillet back on its plate. 'In any case, it's ours now. I think we should slice it in half and, because it seems a bit porky, prepare a sauce whilst the chips cook. Something with cider and apple?'

They put a pan on the hob, adding a slosh of cider vinegar and butter, and overcooking some apple slices before adding them to the sauce. They had experimented with so many meats and cuts now that they did not need to consult recipe books for the accoutrements.

When the sauce was reduced and chips golden and crispy, they sliced the meat in two and heated their steak pan.

'I'm not sure if it is pork,' said William, eyeing the cross-section of the fillet.

'If it is warthog or something, it must look a little different.' Lottie seasoned the cuts and placed a hand over the pan, testing the heat. 'Let's go.'

It sizzled, frying in its own fat till the middle blushed only a little bit red.

'Medium, just like Mr McMurphy said.' Lottie turned off the heat as William served the chips. They drizzled sauce over their meals and brought them to the table.

Each sliced a strip from their fillet and they took their first bites at the same time. Concentration was written on their faces as they tasted and placed the flavour. Lottie swallowed first.

'I'm sure it's pork,' she said. 'It's not a normal pig, but that's the closest thing I can think of.'

'I agree.' William licked his lips. 'It must be some kind of swine. Either a boar or a hog. It's good, isn't it?'

'It is.' Lottie went in for a second bite. 'I've never quite tasted anything like it. We shall have to ask Mr McMurphy what it is when we're next in his shop. I'm sure we're right.'

* * *

But Mr McMurphy did not reveal the source of the mystery meat when Lottie next returned to the shop.

'That would be telling.' He waved a bloodstained fingertip at Lottie. 'And until you get it right, I'm not going to tell you.'

'But it is *some* kind of pig, isn't it? William and I both thought so.'

Mr McMurphy smiled devilishly.

'Not quite. Not quite.' He disappeared for a moment, leaving Lottie to work through a mental checklist of creatures, desperately trying to solve the mystery.

'Is it a foreign animal?' she asked when he reappeared, and a look of amused consideration spread across the butcher's face.

'You know, Lottie, I believe it was from overseas. But that is not to say it's not also indigenous to this country.' He put a large package on the counter before her. 'Here's your second clue.'

Lottie peeked in the top of the bag.

'Wow! It's bigger than those lamb's hearts we tried.'

'So it is. I hope you enjoy.'

'I'm sure we will! The lamb's hearts were delicious. I'm sure this will be too.'

Behind her, the ribbons in the doorway rustled and an old lady pushed her way into the shop with a wicker basket ready for her shopping. Mr McMurphy closed the package in one deft movement and pressed it into Lottie's hands with a quick —

'See you next week then.'

Lottie had removed her purse but the butcher waved her away.

'Thanks very much Lottie. See you soon.'

And Lottie found herself outside the shop with the bulky parcel swinging from one hand.

* * *

'Would you look at that.' William prodded the heart as it sat on a platter. It was the size of two or three of the lambs' hearts, and it smelled more metallic than they had.

'He definitely said it wasn't pig,' said Lottie.

'We'll look in the animal encyclopaedia whilst it cooks.' William watched as a bead of blood dripped from a butchered vein. 'Whatever it is, it deserves something special.'

The encyclopaedia yielded few clues.

'If it is something rare, then we have nothing to compare the taste to,' said Lottie. 'He did say that it came from abroad, but that they could also be found here in Britain.'

'How about a wolf?'

Lottie looked at him.

'I don't think we have wolves here in England anymore.' She flipped the pages of the book. 'It would help if we knew what more parts of it looked like. Maybe Mr McMurphy will give us its trotters or tail or something.'

None the wiser, they removed the seasoned heart from its hours-long spell in the slow cooker. They sliced it in two from top to bottom, so that each had a section of the organ that looked like it could have come from a medical book. They had it with buttered new potatoes and vegetables, with gravy from the heart's cooking poured all over.

'It's interesting,' said William, after chewing for a while. 'But I don't know if it's as good as the lamb's hearts.'

'Maybe we needed to cook it for longer,' said Lottie. 'It feels a bit tougher than the other hearts. Maybe it had a harder life than the lambs – maybe it was a beast of burden.'

'Maybe. I think it tastes just a little...' William ate a potato. 'Bloodier.'

'Yes.' Lottie had eaten more than William, but now she stopped. 'I don't think this one was as tasty as other cuts we've had.'

'Win some, lose some,' said William. They finished what they could, and cleared their plates away.

* * *

'William! I have something for you.' Mr McMurphy rubbed his hands together and dived below the counter, returning with a long coil of sausage. 'Care to hazard any more guesses?'

'Ah...' William blinked nervously. 'We don't know. But we think the heart must have come from a pig-sized creature. You may just need to tell us what it was.'

Mr McMurphy set the coil down.

'Perhaps something in sausage form will prompt your thoughts.'

William looked down at the sausage. It looked innocent enough.

'How does it compare to the heart?' he asked, and something must have shown in his face, for Mr McMurphy's eyes narrowed.

'Did you not care for the heart, William?' His fingers drummed on the butcher's block. 'I saved it for you especially.'

'It was... It was a bold flavour,' said William. 'Perhaps a little too... too bold for myself and Lottie. I think we might have undercooked it,' he finished meekly.

Mr McMurphy gave him a long look.

'Then give this a try,' he said, patting the sausage with the flat of the cleaver that had just appeared in his hand. 'See what you think. Then I might tell you where it comes from.'

He made no move to offer the sausage and William picked it up, slipped it into his bag, and left the shop.

* * *

'He didn't like that we didn't appreciate the heart.' William shrugged at Lottie.

'I suppose it has been the first cut we didn't like.' Lottie looked at the coiled sausage. 'It just didn't feel... *right* to me, somehow. I can't explain it. But I've felt more certain of it ever since last Saturday.'

'I know. I agree.'

'And this from the same animal?' Lottie picked up the sausage. 'There's no way we'll be able to guess it from this.'

'He says he might tell us next week anyway. He seems to like the meat; I think he was disappointed because he had saved the heart for us rather than scoffing it himself.'

'Well... I suppose one more try won't hurt.' Lottie laid out the thick rope of meat. 'But we'll cook this one a little differently.'

They sliced the sausage into discs half an inch thick and fried them off with garlic, onion, mushrooms and peppers, throwing the pan-load into a cheesy pasta sauce. Lottie saved two slices to eat on their own however, and she and William each nibbled tentatively at their morsel as they combined the ingredients of their meal.

'It's alright,' said William. 'It's nice.'

'Yes.' Lottie blinked, as if she had been expecting much worse. 'It is nice. Peppery. Perhaps it was only the heart that tasted strange.'

They ate their pasta with a bottle of wine. William was halfway through his meal when a frown spread across his face. Lottie watched as he chewed around a bit and then, face crumpled, spat out something into his hand.

'What is it?'

William, still frowning, poked at the small, pale item in his palm.

'I don't know. It looks like...' He prodded it again, flipping it over. 'It looks like a bit of tooth.'

Lottie peered at the offending article as William

ran a fingertip round his mouth.

'Is it yours?' Lottie whispered and, after a moment, William shook his head slowly.

'I don't think so. Nothing feels wrong.'

They both stared at his hand.

'It can't be a piece of tooth,' reasoned Lottie. 'Animal teeth don't look like ours. It must just be a little chunk of bone, or a bit of gristle that got disfigured in the mincing machine.'

'You're probably right.' William still did not look happy. 'There's been something odd about this meat though. I don't know if we should be eating it. I really don't. It feels strange.'

'You know what.' Lottie got to her feet. 'Let's get a takeaway.'

'A takeaway?'

'Yes. Something unhealthy, drenched in grease. Something that's made from the scrappiest bits of animals all mashed together. No salad, just chips on the side.'

'That sounds just about right to me,' said William.

When their order was delivered, they lounged on the sofa with the Saturday night movie, a pizza box gaping between them and a carton full of fries shared onto two plates. It tasted as good as any dinner ever had done.

* * *

Neither Lottie nor William paid a visit to Mr McMurphy the next Saturday. It was not a pre-meditated decision; simply, neither expressed a wish to go. When the afternoon rolled past into evening, they booked a table at a restaurant a short walk away and treated themselves to a meal out.

'This is a lovely change.' Lottie had worn her favourite green dress in honour of the spontaneous decision. They clinked their glasses together and ordered their main courses – skipping starters and leaving room for dessert afterward. Both chose something fairly unadventurous – a burger for Lottie and a tuna steak for William.

'I've enjoyed our meat adventure,' said William. 'But I think we've tried about all we ever could.'

'There are loads more meats out there,' said Lottie. 'But I know what you mean. I think we've broadened our horizons, improved our cooking, and given a lot of support to local businesses.'

'I feel now as if we can slow down and perhaps re-try a few of the recipes we really loved, rather than sprinting on to something different.' William paused as their plates were set before them by a young waitress, and for a few minutes neither spoke as they enjoyed their own individual meals. The restaurant was cosy. The nights were getting longer, but it was a clear and pretty night.

'I do wonder though,' said William, 'what that mysterious meat was. It was probably the most obscure meat we tried. The rarest cut.'

'We'll ask Mr McMurphy next week,' said Lottie. 'Because we'll still be eating meat, and I still want to buy it from such a good butcher. Even if we mainly go for beef and chicken and pork and lamb from now on, instead of strange creatures.'

After their mains, Lottie ordered a sticky toffee pudding and William had a chocolate fudge cake. Afterwards, they strolled home at a leisurely pace, breath misting a little in the bracing air.

* * *

William pulled his coat on.

'Just some mince then?'

'Yep.' Lottie saw him to the front door. 'Lamb mince. We'll have a shepherd's pie for tea.'

'Sounds good to me.' William swung the door shut behind him.

Lottie knew William would not be gone for long, and flicked the television on to idle in the background. She half-watched a cooking show as she tidied around the living room.

The cooking programme finished, to be replaced with another one, featuring a brash American eating huge sandwiches. Lottie aimed the remote and found a nature documentary. But when this too finished she frowned, and looked at the clock.

Where was William? He should have been back by now.

Lottie put her phone to her ear, but there was

no dial tone and the call went straight to voicemail. Lottie did not leave one. His phone must have run out of battery, that was all. She was not worried – William liked a good stroll, and might have just taken a detour into town.

She waited half-hour as concern rose in her tummy, drumming her fingers on the arm of the settee. When yet another thirty minutes had passed, she got to her feet. She wrote a little note in her pad and propped it up so that William would see it if he came in:

Just out looking for you. Give me a ring if you get in before me.

Then she pulled on her boots and coat and set out.

It was not a long walk to Mr McMurphy's butcher's shop – perhaps twenty-five minutes. They tended to drive if they were stocking up their freezer, but for odd bits they either walked or cycled. William had walked today, citing the wander as an opportunity to listen to a new record he had downloaded. Lottie kept an eye out as she wandered towards the butcher's shop in case William was to pass on the other side of the street. But she did not see him.

She arrived at Mr McMurphy's all warm from her walk, and rustled past the hanging ribbons in his doorway.

The shopfront was empty, but that was not unusual. The butcher was often in his back room preparing his wares. A radio, perched on a high shelf, played Radio 4. Lottie dinged the bell on the counter and waited for Mr McMurphy.

It took nearly two minutes for the butcher to appear. He was dressed in his apron. The red patches on it seemed shiny and fresh.

'Good afternoon Mr McMurphy.'

'Good afternoon Lottie.' Mr McMurphy paused a moment, as if weighing his words. His face was not as smiley as it usually was. 'What can I get for you today?'

'Actually, I was just popping in to see if William had been in to see you. He was on his way here, but he's been gone ages.' She spotted a flash of recognition in the butcher's face, and Mr McMurphy saw that she saw it.

'Yes,' he said, and paused again. 'Yes, he was here earlier.'

Lottie noticed the handle of Mr McMurphy's favoured cleaver sticking out of one of his pockets.

'When was that? Did he say where he was going?'

'He hadn't visited for a couple of weeks,' said the butcher. 'He said he didn't much like the last package I gave him.'

'We... We're just ready for something a bit more normal now,' said Lottie. 'He was here, then? He did buy something and leave?'

'He still couldn't guess what the meat was,' said Mr McMurphy. His thumb kneaded the handle of his cleaver unconsciously.

'We couldn't place it,' said Lottie. 'And we still

don't know. I think I'll have to go now though, Mr McMurphy. I'm sure William can't have gone far, but I need to find him.'

'Oh,' said Mr McMurphy. 'But he's here. In the back room. I wanted to show him what the meat was.'

'He's still here?'

'Yes indeed.' The butcher opened an arm, inviting Lottie round the counter. She padded across the shop, across the sawdusted floor, past the rows of fillets and steaks and strings of sausages. 'Yes, he was very surprised when he discovered what he had been eating these past weeks. And you know: that surprise quite made up for the fact that you and he kept away for so long.'

'It was only a week,' said Lottie, and she stepped through the butcher's door into the back room. 'William? Where are you?' She could see a dark shape at the back of the room, but Mr McMurphy had turned all the lights off, and she couldn't tell what it was. 'Is that you?'

'That's him,' said Mr McMurphy. Lottie hadn't realised how close he'd got to her, how his cleaver had leapt into his hand, how his apron smelled so strongly of fresh meat. 'William is just helping me with my latest batch of rare cuts. Won't you join him?'

THE GOBLIN HUNT

'No, no. That's much too short; you won't be able to catch one with that.'

Nanna watched as Christopher frowned and threw the stick back on the pile. Then he bent down to tug at a larger branch, his little hands wrapped around the thick stick. There were already half-moons of muck under his nails; they'd only been here two minutes.

'That's better…' Nanna surveyed the stick as Christopher beamed up at her. It was good and stout and around three feet long. In the five-year-old's hand it looked the size of a walking cane or staff. 'Better, but not perfect.'

'Oh…' Christopher looked at the stick. 'Why not?'

Nanna pointed at the end of it.

'A perfect stick should have a V-shape on the end.'

Christopher's bright blue eyes lit up.

'To hook a goblin!'

'Exactly.'

He dived back to the woodpile, rummaging through the offcuts of branches and bushes.

Nanna smiled at him and shuffled her feet. It was autumn, and it was getting colder. But the last few nights had been mostly dry – only the odd shower of rain had hissed outside her window at night – and the morning felt fresh. The grass underfoot felt springy, and the disturbed pile of timber gave off a resiny, wholesome scent. The sun was shining, and a few clouds soared high overhead. It was a perfect day for a goblin hunt.

'Nanna, look!'

Christopher was brandishing a new stick. It was slightly larger than the last one; a branch from a big oak tree perhaps. It was bent at a couple of points, but was mostly straight. And most importantly, it ended with two prongs of twigs that formed a V, one twig slightly longer than the other.

'Let me see.' Nanna took the stick and looked it over, then handed it back to Christopher with reverence. 'It's a very fine goblin stick. You look after it, now.'

Christopher thumped the stick into the ground a couple of times.

'Shall we go and look for goblins now?'

'Oh yes. Now that we have our stick.'

Nanna held out a hand, and Christopher took it. His hand felt very small and smooth. Nanna smiled.

It was also cold and dirty from poking in the woodpile.

They set off back to the path. The pile was in the back of a churchyard, near a gardener's shed surrounded by a scattering of empty flowerpots. The shed and pots looked almost like a miniature diorama of the church itself, with its constellations of headstones.

'Where do the goblins live, Nanna?'

Christopher was thumping his stick on the pathway with every step.

'In the woods.' Nanna knew which woods to take him to.

They passed through an avenue of pollarded yew trees, trunks corrugated and stripped of leaves. A few berries lay on the ground, some unbroken, some pulped by the stomping of feet. When they reached the lychgate, Christopher fumbled with the latch and held it open for Nanna.

'Thank you, sweetheart.'

'You're welcome.'

Christopher's voice was practiced; polite. He pulled the gate to, and reached his arm over to make sure the latch had caught. He set off at trot, but Nanna caught him and took his hand. For a few minutes, they would be walking by the side of the road.

They passed over a bridge before they reached the pedestrian crossing, and Nanna let Christopher push the button to call the traffic to a halt. He jumped from white stripe to white stripe and made it safely to the bobbly red tiles on the other side, stick knocking irregularly on the ground.

The woods were only a mile or so from the house. For every step Nanna took, Christopher took two, his little legs scurrying, full of energy. Nanna hadn't let her pace slow as she'd grown older, and was still capable of the long strides she'd taken in her youth.

'What will we do when we find a goblin?' asked Christopher, waving his stick. They turned away from the road and started down a narrower road that would lead them to the forest.

'Well, you'll have to catch it.' Nanna let go of Christopher as he whizzed the stick forward in a two-handed grip.

'And then what?'

Nanna smiled. Then what? She had an image come to her mind's eye: goblin hunting for sport. She imagined Christopher's Granda catching a goblin with his fishing rod, weighing it in his hands and then throwing it back into the woods to dart away between the trees, rubbing its cheek.

'I suppose we'd have to let it go. I don't think your mum would let you keep a goblin.'

The path was becoming gravelly and clotted with fallen leaves. Bushes rose up on either side.

'Why not? We could keep it in Anne's room –' Anne was Christopher's sister – 'and feed it... feed it...'

'Custard,' said Nanna. 'Goblins love custard.' She held his hand again as they crossed the treeline and entered the woods.

Christopher held her hand for a few seconds

before disengaging and running off down the path. His blonde hair caught the sun as it filtered through the rusty leaves and twigs, and it shone.

'Careful,' warned Nanna. Her eyes didn't leave him as he sprinted ahead, jumping over roots and poking at rabbit holes with the goblin stick.

The woods felt pleasant. The ground was a little muddy, but nothing their wellies couldn't handle, and the light rains of the previous nights had released the scents of the place. Trees, leafy mulch, wet ferns. Around them, twigs crackled and leaves whispered, whether in the breeze or as small animals made their way through the trees. Nanna smiled. Perhaps some of the scurrying sounds were goblins.

She caught up with Christopher as he stood on his tip toes, peering into a hollow knot in an elm tree.

'Have you found one, sweetheart?'

'No. I thought there might be custard in there.' Christopher lowered himself down and poked at the hollow with his stick. 'We could put some in there as a trap.'

'To lure a goblin. Very clever.'

'Why do they like custard so much?'

Nanna thought for a moment.

'Well, it's very tasty. Wouldn't you be tempted by a nice big bowl of custard?'

Christopher's eyes crinkled as he thought about it.

'Yes.'

'Well, there you go.'

They continued on their way. Christopher kept closer now, stick thumping on the ground, squelching as it hit more waterlogged parts of the path. The woods were quiet. Apart from the sounds of nature, there were no other noises: no other footsteps or coughs of other walkers, no barks of dogs. Even the traffic was far away and muted behind a shield of trees. A passing aeroplane, visible through the trees above, reminded Nanna that they hadn't wandered into some hidden realm.

'Look Nanna!'

Christopher was pointing up. To their right, the woods rose up at a steep gradient – they were following the path round the base of a hill. Christopher was staring up at the ridge.

'What have you seen, my love?'

'I think it was a goblin!' Christopher remembered his stick and brandished it.

'Goodness me. We'll have to be on our guard. We wouldn't to be hunted *by* a goblin.'

'Why not?' Christopher was still staring up the top of the hill, blue eyes raking back and forth. Nanna wondered if he'd seen a dogwalker, or just a suspect tree from the corner of his eye. 'We could let it follow us, and hide, and jump out, and, and catch it...'

'Well, goblins are mischievous,' said Nanna. They started to walk again, plumbing further into the woods. 'They might want to steal you, and make you live with them.'

'Wow!' Christopher spun around on the spot –

to have so much energy! thought Nanna – and jumped onto a nearby rock before hopping back off again. 'Living with goblins.'

'I can't imagine it would be that nice,' said Nanna. She thought of stories of changelings and lost babes in the woods. Of grandmothers and wolves and breadcrumb trails. 'Goblins live in dark places, like caves and drains. You wouldn't want to live there when you have your mum, and your dad, and Anne.'

'*Anne* could live with the goblins!' Christopher waved his stick.

'She's much too little to live with goblins.'

'They might gobble her up!'

'And you would have to protect her, as her big brother.'

Nanna let Christopher bounce ahead, always keeping his blue coat in sight. She wondered for how long he would want to come goblin-hunting with her; how long before he wouldn't want to hold her hand as they walked. Having a grandchild was special – it was like reliving having her own children all over again. Though without quite so much responsibility. It sounded strange to think it, but children only got older – not younger. At any one time, they were as young as they were ever going to be.

Christopher zoomed back to her.

'When we've hunted goblins, can we have sticky buns?'

'Oh, I should think so.'

'Yay!' Christopher scanned the woods in search

of their quarry. 'And when I'm grown up, I can take you for sticky buns instead.'

Nanna reached out and stroked his hair.

'Don't grow up too quickly,' she said.

They tramped on down the path. Nanna knew the vague shape of these woods, but not the intricacies of the paths; she only visited every few months. But they'd only been strolling for fifteen minutes or so. She liked to think they could make it to half an hour before Christopher got restless and they headed into the town for the promised buns.

There was a rustle in the trees to their right and Nanna peered through the forest, eyes flicking over tree trunks, leaf piles and mossy rocks. Nothing. A woodland creature, startled from its nest by their presence and now hiding, frozen, in the undergrowth.

'Nanna?'

'Yes, dear?'

'Do all goblins look the same?'

'Well,' said Nanna. 'Not necessarily. Some are small and green, with yellow eyes, pointy noses and sharp little teeth. But some can be big and fat.'

'From the custard,' breathed Christopher.

Nanna bit back a smile.

'Yes. And some can disguise themselves as people.'

'What about, what about trolls. They're like big goblins.'

'Some trolls are hairy but some can have scales, and they are often stupid. They live under bridges.'

'Like the billy goats gruff.'

'They met a troll when they crossed a bridge.'

'I think I saw a goblin, Nanna.'

'Did you, sweetheart? Just now?'

'Yeah.' Christopher peered round at the forest around them. 'It was... small, like a little boy size, and it had a light green face and, and yellow eyes, and a little hat on.'

'Did it really? Was this up on the hill?'

'No, in the forest. It was looking out from behind a tree.'

'Goodness me.' Nanna looked around. 'We shall have to be careful. Have you got your stick ready, in case it jumps out at us?'

'Yes, I have.' Christopher held the stick in two hands, ready to jab towards a goblin.

'Well, you keep tight hold of it. And we can catch the goblin together.'

They kept walking. Christopher was very imaginative. Nanna liked to think a goblin hunt was good for a child. It encouraged imagination, and fresh air and walking. Much better than the handheld electronic games she saw children with nowadays. Maybe when Christopher was grown up he would still like walking in the woods, mind's eye busy picturing goblins and ghouls. Maybe he would use that imagination; paint pictures or write books – he was good at school, after all, and he read voraciously. When he was old enough she could introduce him to her library of Stephen King paperbacks.

He was running on ahead now. The path had been following the curve of the hill; Nanna felt sure they were only ten minutes or so from making a full circle and emerging from the woods. But for now, the trees were still plentiful, and the bushes dense. A thick stratum of leaves squelched underfoot. She had to increase her pace to catch sight of Christopher as he explored further down the path, and off into the trees to either side.

'Careful, sweetheart. I can't take you home all muddy.'

She heard a gleeful '*wheee!*' ahead as Christopher zoomed around. She'd take him for sticky buns soon, and then they'd make their way back to the house. Goblinless, but full of fresh air and perhaps a little worn out, ready for an afternoon on the sofa.

She thought of his description of the goblin he had seen. She wondered where he'd had the idea for a hat. The weather was colder; people had started to wear them more. Perhaps he had noticed that on their walk to the churchyard.

'Christopher?'

Nanna quickened her pace. He had run off ahead, and around the curve of the path, out of sight. It was nothing to worry about; she knew it was unlikely that any mishap could befall him just around the next corner. But losing sight of him still sent a pang of worry through her belly. She wouldn't want him to trip over and get all dirty, at the very least.

She rounded the corner; the path straightened

a little. She could see the forest with little impediment, but there was no blue coat amongst the trees.

'Christopher? Are you hiding?' Nanna looked around. He must be behind a tree or bush. He was hiding; waiting to leap out and give her a fright. 'Christopher! Where have you got to?'

Nanna turned around, in case she had already passed his hiding place, but he was nowhere to be seen. She whipped around and started forward, and when she called his name again she heard a note of panic in her own voice, which she tried to quell. She didn't want to alarm him; just make him come out.

The forest seemed murkier, suddenly. When the sun dipped behind clouds, the gaps between trees seemed to shrink. The twigs and branches overhead formed a denser canopy, and ferns and bushes reached out over the path to brush Nanna as she paced ahead, wellies sticky on the ground. The hill loomed over to her right; to her left, the woods rustled and lurked, all leafy ground and tendrilly branches.

'Christopher? Christopher?'

Panic was a useless emotion, but it was unthinkable that she could lose Christopher, her daughter's son, her grandson...

'Christopher!'

There he was. In the trees to her right, his blue coat visible amongst the trunks and twigs.

Nanna slowed her pace. Already the panic was ebbing, leaving an urge to tell him off for putting her through such worry. But she swallowed it down.

'Christopher, you shouldn't run off like that. I didn't know where you were. I was worried...'

Christopher turned at her words, and started to stomp back to the path. When he got there, she pulled him into a cuddle that was a little tighter than necessary.

'I was worried,' she said again. She took his hand and they continued down the path.

They were nearly at the end of the route now. Christopher wasn't speaking, and his steps had lost their bounce. Nanna worried that her words had sounded too stern.

'Nearly there now,' she said. 'We can head into a nice cafe and have ourselves a sticky bun. You'll have to leave...' she looked down at Christopher. 'What happened to your goblin stick?'

Christopher looked down, then up at her.

'I dropped it. In the trees.'

'Well, we would have had to leave it behind anyway. Goblins sticks can't really come into coffee shops.'

Christopher didn't reply.

'Did you see any goblins in the trees?'

Nanna gave his hand a little squeeze.

'No.'

'Oh.'

Nanna glanced around at the trees. She could see the end of the path ahead; the little sign denoting the public bridleway. Yes, it was nice to have Christopher for the morning; to relive having her own children again. But all that love had a flipside; it became so much worry if anything unplanned happened.

'I'm sorry to have told you off,' she said. 'I was worried that you'd got lost. I've only got one grandson; I can't have him getting lost. And what would your mum say if I'd lost you in goblin-infested woods?'

Above, the sun edged out from behind the white fluffy clouds. Christopher looked up at Nanna. The sun caught his face and turned his blonde hair white. His eyes looked pale, reflecting the yellow sun.

'It's okay,' he said. His hand felt warm in hers. They reached the bridleway sign and stepped out of the forest, onto a track leading back to the town centre.

'Lovely. I think it's time for a cup of coffee for me, and a Coca-Cola for you. What kind of sticky bun would you like?'

Christopher looked up at her again.

'Something with custard,' he said.

And they wandered on towards town, their goblin hunt complete.

UNDER THE OAK

'I understand why you won't talk to me.'

Jamie leaned back against the trunk of the oak and looked over at Jess. She didn't meet his gaze. The evening breeze blew a few strands of copper hair across her cheek.

'I do,' said Jamie. 'I do understand. I know that I did a bad thing. Something that I shouldn't have done. But – Jess – you did something bad first, you know? What I did was because of that.'

Jamie closed his eyes. This was difficult. He'd always found it difficult to talk about his feelings. Even – no, especially – when it was with a loved one. He knotted his fingers around a corner of the picnic blanket.

'I don't know how long it had been going on,' he started. 'Between you and Jason. But do you know when I found out? My birthday. My birthday, Jess. John told me, John from the cinema. He saw you with

Jason, saw you kissing.'

Jess didn't reply. The sun was low in the sky, but the night was still warm. Jamie brushed a sheen of sweat from his brow and opened his eyes.

'I knew when you came around that night. The presents you gave me hurt me. I knew you weren't giving them with love anymore. No –' he pointed at Jess. 'Don't deny it. You didn't love me anymore, and I knew it for fact.' He tugged at the blanket again. 'But I didn't let you know. Not then. That's why I wanted to meet you today. To talk about our feelings. To... to end it, I suppose.'

He hauled himself to his knees and knelt in front of Jess.

'I am sorry for what I've done. I didn't mean to. But it's done, and I'm sorry.'

He looked into her eyes. The rigor mortis was already setting in, and it twitched her lip into something like a smile of forgiveness. He smiled back.

'Bye Jess.'

He finished rolling her in the blanket, mopped his brow and readied his spade. It was a warm summer's night under the oak.

RED CHRISTMAS

Bertie's night was not going to plan.

He'd meant to have the place to himself tonight. Send the others home just after the end-of-day bell, leaving him alone with aisle upon aisle of merchandise, carefully stocked and catalogued by his team in Warehouse Three.

Well. Carefully catalogued for the most part. Some of the gear here had evaded the stock check by hiding in huge, wrapped parcels, or by being tactically shunted around the place ahead of the guys with the checklist. Some of the stuff had been written off as water-damaged – there had been a hole in the roof for years, not that the snow ever got in at a volume large enough to seriously mess anything up.

Bertie had parked his wagon at the loading doors, ready to liberate those products that had fallen off the grid in favour of more lucrative transactions in the new year. He had not counted on the presence of

Tillie.

He made his way back to the manager's office – his office – and leant against the door. He motioned with the mug of hot chocolate in his hand. Well, it was nearly Christmas.

'You should get yourself home. You don't need to stay – I've got this all wrapped up.'

Tillie looked up. She was always pale and there was a perennial blush about her cheeks which complemented the green of her standard-issue uniform.

'I'm okay. I'd rather stay now and not have this hanging over my head.' She was holding a clipboard in one hand and burrowing through a stack of documents on the desk with the other. Bertie scowled at the back of her head, where blonde hair spilled out from under her cap.

'Honestly,' he said. 'I can hold the fort. In a couple of weeks this place will be heaving, day and night. Right up to Christmas Eve. We'll all be pulling all-nighters then. You should make the most of having some time for yourself.'

'I've got no plans.' Tillie brushed a lock of hair behind a pointed ear without looking at Bertie. 'And I'd rather get this out the way. You know there are discrepancies in the counts in some of the other depots? Artie's place is getting a visit from the boss. He's bricking it.'

'The guvnor is speaking to Artie about stock?'

'That's what Freddie says. He's the

development coordinator there.'

Bertie licked his lips, his mouth suddenly dry. He took a swig of hot chocolate. The marshmallow that he had melted into it earlier had gone to jelly, and he scraped a curd of it off the rim of the mug with his teeth.

'Well, we've got nothing to worry about here,' he said, keeping his voice neutral. 'I run a tight ship. Never missed a consignment. There are damages – always are, especially with Millie on the forklift. But nothing that should involve getting Big Nick down here to investigate.'

Tillie did not answer, only ran a pencil down a list in front of her on the desk.

'I do have plans for tonight,' said Bertie, changing tack. 'Actually. I'm meeting some of the other managers for a quick pow-wow before things start hotting up this season. So, I should be leaving soon.'

'That's okay, Bertie. You can leave the keys with me. I can lock up when I'm all done.'

'Ah. No. You see, I can't have you unattended here in the warehouse. The only member of personnel who's authorised to be on their own is the manager. So, I guess that means I'll have to send you on your way before I'm allowed to leave.' *Then I'll let you go on ahead – I've got a few things to tie up before I'm off for the night. Promises to keep. Deals to honour.*

Tillie chewed a strand of her hair.

'Okay. But can we just check something quickly? I'm sure there's something on this list that's missing. It's the kind of thing the guvnor will jump straight on if he sees it.'

'Fine. Let's just make it quick.' Bertie drained his mug and set it down on the desk as Tillie led him out of the office and onto the warehouse floor. They were climbing the stairs when Bertie heard a sound. He grabbed Tillie's arm and she halted.

'What?'

'Shhh.'

Bertie could feel his ears twitching as they strained to hear it again. It had been – what? A high-pitched sound. A squeak, maybe. Rats?

'What?'

Tillie was looking at him. He shook his head.

'I thought I heard something. Must have just been the wind. The hole in the roof...'

'We seem to lose a lot of product because of that hole. We should get it fixed.'

'So I keep telling them...'

Bertie grinned to himself, the sudden chill he had felt dissipating. That hole was the gift that kept on giving. No way was that going to get fixed whilst it let him shift so much stock out the back door.

The stairs led up to the mezzanine floor. There was a cage at the back for high-value items. Electronics, batteries, the modern stuff. You had to be careful with how much of that you wrote off, especially since the hole in the roof was at the other end of the warehouse. Tillie was making for the cage.

'You have the keys?' she said.

Bertie patted the pockets of his waistcoat.

'Still on the hook.' He shrugged. 'I didn't know you needed them.'

Tillie's face flashed with something Bertie couldn't immediately recognise. Annoyance? Triumph? His blood ran cold.

She's onto me, he thought. *I don't know when she found out, but she did. She knows I'm doing something I shouldn't.*

But Tillie's face was back to normal.

'We can just grab them and come back,' she said. 'It'll only take a minute. Bertie?'

But Bertie was staring past her, out through the snow-dusted windows into the night beyond. He raised an arm, pointed a finger.

'What...?'

Tillie turned, and Bertie heard a soft intake of breath.

Somewhere, out there in the complex, a building was on fire.

Tillie stepped closer to the window. Bertie could see her breath misting the pane. He had no idea what had caused the fire, but his mind was already racing. He had never kept the tidiest of warehouses – a little mess was an effective smokescreen for his occasional skimming of merchandise – and suddenly a length of red-and-white-painted four-by-two had found its way into his hand. A smart whack on the back of the head, and he could be free of Tillie for the night. He could drag her down below the hole in the roof, that good old gift that kept on giving, and make it look like it had fallen in on her. It would buy him some time. Give her a warning, too, about messing with his affairs.

But Bertie had never given anyone a whack on the head before. How hard would he need to do it? He didn't want to kill the meddling shrew, just knock her out for a spell. His grip tightened on the spar. His mouth was dry again and the taste of hot chocolate had turned bitter on his tongue.

'Bertie,' said Tillie, before he could raise his weapon. 'That's Warehouse One. Warehouse One is on fire.'

Warehouse One. The one which had started it all. It made Bertie's domain look like a store cupboard. Warehouse One was connected to the factory floor, and the stables. The guvnor had his rooms there as well, up and away from the bustle of construction and packing. Once, there had only been Warehouse One, and it was known only as the Workshop. That was before Bertie's time. But the enterprise had been forced to expand; there was too much demand from all around the world.

Bertie joined Tillie at the window.

'Listen,' he said.

The fire had lit the snow around the complex with an orange glow. Bertie could hear it – a crackling sound, like paper being scrunched. Something else too, a deeper sound. The wooden structure of the building groaning as the heat worked on its skeleton, forcing beams and timbers to expand and push against each other.

'What's happened out there?' he said out loud.

'Shhh.' Tillie was listening, one pointed ear twitching towards the sound. Then Bertie heard it too. The sound he had mistaken for the squeak of rats in the building.

Screams.

'We have to help them.' Tillie was already moving. 'I saw your wagon at the back door. We should...' she tailed off. Bertie saw that her eyes were fixed on the length of four-by-two in his hand.

'Y-yes,' he stammered, raising the spar as if he had just picked it up. 'We've got to help in any way we can.'

Tillie eyed the spar and stepped back.

'Why are you holding that?' she said.

Bertie hesitated and, in that moment, Tillie's face flashed again. Before Bertie could react, she stepped forward and swung the curly-toed tip of her boot up into Bertie's crotch. He dropped the spar and collapsed to his knees, gasping as a glowing, winded sensation spread up through his core.

'You bastard,' hissed Tillie. Then she was gone, a streak of green and blonde disappearing down the stairs.

Bertie scrunched his eyes closed against the pain and spat out a curse. When he opened his eyes tears of pain were tracking down his face. A moment later he heard a rattling, coughing sound. The motor of his wagon. She was stealing it. Why had he left the keys on the hook instead of keeping them in his pocket?

Slowly, Bertie got to his feet. There were two baubles of dull pain between his legs, and he tried not to bump them as he bent for his spar and staggered to the stairs.

He had to follow her. The jig was up, and she'd be pinning attempted assault on him now too. He wasn't well liked in the warehouse – the new guys, they didn't get what it meant to be an old-school manager. They didn't get how things used to work. He had to get to her and silence her. Bribe her, put the scare on her. Whatever it took. His associates were not so amenable as he, and if they found out he'd let the cat out of the bag...

He hobbled, using his spar for support. His wagon had been parked round the back, but he could cut out that segment of the journey by leaving through the front door. When he opened up the double doors, he saw the distinctive pattern of wheel and ski-marks in the snow that were the signature tracks of his wagon. All he had to do was follow those tracks.

Bertie took a step outside. The ache in his belly was fading, slowly. He just had to put it from his mind. He looked up.

Glowing embers floated on the breeze, ahead of the screams. The very air was different to how it should have been – not sterile and snow-filtered but warm and smoky. Not the smoke of a cosy log fire but the smoke of burning hopes and dreams.

Bertie set off along the tracks scored into the

snow by the wagon. He still didn't quite know what to do when he found Tillie. Maybe she'd get herself hurt in the blaze anyway, and he wouldn't have to do a thing. And speaking of the blaze, what had caused that? Bertie had never seen so much fire in his life. A log fire that had gotten out of control? An electrical fault? He thought the guvnor had systems in place to prevent this from happening.

Part of him didn't want to follow the tracks. Tillie was a do-gooder. She would be heading straight into the inferno, doing her best to help. That meant following her toward the fire. Risking his own life.

Aren't you risking it anyway? By not delivering the goods?

Yes, he was. But the fire was the definition of exceptional circumstances. His friends would realise that. Besides, without the wagon, he had no way of shifting the gear anyway. Another reason to follow Tillie.

As he neared the burning building Bertie became conscious of the heat of it. It was like sitting uncomfortably close to a log fire – only he was still halfway across the complex. It would be unbearable up close. He wasn't built to suffer heat; none of them were. As he watched, part of the building collapsed – a square timber tower, topped with a pennant which was itself engulfed in flames. It fell out of sight, into where Bertie knew there was an atrium at the heart of building. The rest of Warehouse One was stone-built – it should survive a little longer.

What could have caused such an accident?

Bertie's belly still ached. He stopped in the shadow of Warehouse Two, Artie's place, the one where the guvnor had noticed stock go missing, and rested up against the wall. He swore under his breath in frustration.

He could see signs of life by Warehouse One. There had never been a serious accident here, so there were no ambulances, but he could see the distinctive shape of a first-aid wagon out of range of the blaze. Green-clad figures, silhouetted black against the flames, clustered around the little vehicle with its trailer-mounted apothecary's cabinet on the back.

There won't be enough medicine, thought Bertie. *Those things are for minor injuries. A slipped chisel, a scald from a fumbled mug. You can't put a plaster on a body-sized burn.*

Bertie squinted. Was that – his wagon? Beyond the first-aid trailer? It was! It was hard to tell with it being parked so close to the blaze, but he would recognise its sleek contours anywhere. Tillie had stopped to make herself useful to the injured. The do-good, meddling –

Bertie heaved himself off the wall and trudged on through the snow. He had expected more figures to have congregated outside Warehouse One, but none seemed to be coming. Perhaps they were trapped. Perhaps they were already dead? He had to be careful here. Had to look out for number one.

His eyes scanned the assembly. Some were laying in the snow whilst others stared back at the inferno. Some had blood on their green uniforms, the contrasting colours obscenely festive. Where was –

There! She had someone on her shoulder, was helping them hobble towards the first-aid wagon. Bertie's eyes narrowed. Time to take on Tillie. He started towards her.

Suddenly, a sound tore through the air. Bertie halted. It was like nothing he had heard; a deep, throaty bellow that echoed round the complex. He had heard the howls of wolves before, even the roars of polar bears when they got too close to the complex and had to be chased away. But nothing like this. It did not seem natural, that sound. It had sadness in it, and wrath.

The bellow stopped as suddenly as it had started, leaving a ringing in Bertie's ears. As he watched, the figures around the first-aid wagon started to run, scattering towards him and off to the sides, as if they had just seen some emerging menace approach from behind. Bertie was taking no chances, not after hearing that howl. He limped off towards Warehouse Two. He knew Artie's secret way inside, the way he used to transfer gear out on the sly. One of the wall panels was false and swung like a door. Bertie threw himself against the wall and began banging on panel after panel, seeking signs of movement. He glanced behind him.

A dark shape moved against the burning warehouse. It was indistinct, close enough to the flames that Bertie could see only shadow, and yet it did not burn. It had four legs –

Bertie yelled out loud. He was falling backwards, and he landed with a smack that pumped fresh waves of agony through his abdomen. He looked up.

'Artie!'

Artie ignored him. He appeared to be muttering to himself, a non-stop litany under his breath. But he had opened the secret panel – Bertie was in Warehouse Two, safe from the shape outside. When Artie closed the door, the sensory assault of the fire halted, and Bertie could hear Artie's voice.

'Ohgosh,ohgosh,ohgosh,ohgosh...'

Bertie heaved himself to his feet.

'Artie. Snap out of it. Artie.'

Artie looked at him with glazed eyes.

'Artie.'

Bertie needed no further encouragement. He slapped Artie with an open palm, harder than was perhaps necessary.

Artie's eyes slowly focused behind wire-framed spectacles. His lips stilled, even as a dark, hand-shaped bruise began to colour his cheek. He reached up and adjusted his cap where it had been knocked askew.

'Bertie. It is you.'

'Of course it's me. Who else would it be?'

'You're not the only one who knows about the door. Our friends...' Artie trailed off.

'Artie. What's going on? Do you know what caused the fire?'

Artie's eyes, on their way to glazing once again, suddenly met Bertie's.

'The fire,' he said, and horror spread across his features. 'We need to find somewhere safe.'

'Artie. Wait.'

But Artie was already fleeing. Bertie hauled himself after him and they ran down an aisle of floor-to-ceiling shelves, each shelf laden with wrapped presents, ready for the big delivery.

Artie was making for the manager's office. Bertie caught him before he could slam the door, stealing inside with him. For a moment, both caught their breath in the dark.

Bertie felt nauseated. Tillie's kick combined with the exertion of running – he felt like he was going to throw up. He clenched his fists and found the length of four-by-two still in his hand. He'd kept a grip on it all this time.

'Artie. What's going on?'

Almost imperceptibly, he saw Artie's face move in the darkness. Above them, the timbers of Warehouse Two creaked.

'I couldn't believe it at first.' Artie's voice came through the darkness, weak and faltering. 'I never thought... never believed...'

'Never believed what?'

'I never believed... I never thought he would finally snap. None of us did. But it's him – the freak, Bertie. It's him that did this.'

'No. He can't be capable of all this.'

'It was him. I saw it. My own eyes...'

'How?' Bertie kept a grip on his spar. He reached up, feeling for a lantern, and slowly rolled the dial between his forefinger and thumb. Low orange light filled the office. It reminded him of the colour of Warehouse One, all wreathed in flame. His stomach turned, and he swallowed caustic acid back down.

'I was in there, Bertie. In the workshop. Someone came rushing in, said there had been a commotion out in the stables. Next thing I knew there was fire – people screaming – people dead...'

'The freak did this? Even the fire? How?'

'I don't know. Some flash of red light and then...' Artie's spectacles reflected miniature lanterns. 'Fire. Death.'

They fell silent.

'I never thought it would happen,' said Artie again. 'Never thought he'd do anything. He just always took it, you know? Stood there and took it.'

'Sometimes there's no way of knowing what's going on under the surface.' Bertie thought of how diligently he had hidden his hustle all these years. How Tillie had hidden her knowledge of what he was doing. 'They ostracised him. Made him a pariah. No one knew what he was thinking. None of us knows what it must feel like, alone, cut off from everybody else. To live with so much cruelty.'

'They used to laugh and call him names,' said Artie. 'And so did we. We called him the freak. Never gave him a chance...'

'Did he plan it, you think?'

'I don't know.'

'He might have planned this. If he had power we all knew nothing about – maybe he trained, made himself stronger.'

'Or maybe he did just... snap.'

Bertie clutched his spar. It would take more than a smart whack to put the freak down.

'We could run,' he said. 'Take a wagon and ride.'

'Ride where, Bertie?' Artie's voice was shaking a little. 'It's only ice, for miles around. Glaciers and snow. We'd freeze to death out there.'

Bertie cursed. 'Then what are we meant to do? Just hide? I –'

But Artie had jumped on him, and clasped a tiny hand over his mouth.

'Shhh,' he hissed, lips close to Bertie's ear. 'He's here.'

Bertie's body froze. He was conscious of the beating of his heart, strong in his chest. Slowly, Artie removed his hand from Bertie's mouth and pointed.

'There,' he mouthed.

A window ran around three walls of the office, a wide array of glass that let the manager see out into the warehouse beyond. Bertie and Artie were on the floor, below the level of the window. They were out of sight. But Bertie could see what Artie was pointing at. A red glow had appeared at one end of the window. As Bertie watched, it began to move. It was as if someone were holding a red lightbulb and walking with it, unhurriedly, across the warehouse floor.

'It's him,' he whispered, and Artie shoved a panicked hand against his mouth again.

Now that Bertie listened, he could hear the soft clopping of furry hooves on the stone floor. His breath stopped as they grew louder, the red light growing stronger in the middle of the office window. Then he breathed as the sounds moved off, and the light grew dimmer. Artie let go of his face.

'What does he want from us?' whispered Bertie.

'What would you want?' hissed Artie. 'Revenge. Now that he's started, he won't stop until we're all dead or he is.'

The red glow had vanished. Slowly, Bertie stood up and looked out of the window. The aisles were empty and dark.

'Someone's onto me,' he said, after a beat. 'A woman. Tillie. She rumbled my operation.'

'Tillie? She used to work in here.'

'Then she's the one that rumbled you.'

'No one's rumbled me. I'm safe as houses.'

'No. The guvnor's onto you. You got a development manager? Eddie?'

'Freddie.'

'Him. I think he worked with Tillie to grass you up. Big Nick's coming your way. Or was.'

'Rather him than our friends.'

'Would you?' Bertie paused. 'I don't know.

He's a powerful man, Artie. I wouldn't want to end up on his naughty list.'

'Perhaps this could work out to our advantage.' Artie stood and crept to the door. 'I want out, Bertie. Have done for years. It's too much risk for too little pay-out. But if the freak takes down our friends, it's problem solved.'

'You think the guvnor can do it? Stop the freak?'

Artie shrugged.

'You said it yourself. He's a powerful man. He's got a kind of magic, doesn't he? He might be able to rein him in.'

'If he's not already dead.'

Bertie's mouth spat the words out even before he'd realised he was thinking them. Maybe that had been his rooms up there in the wooden tower he'd seen topple over? The chambers the guvnor shared with his wife? If Big Nick was dead, that was a dimension all of its own. No need to catch Tillie any longer – she wouldn't have anyone to report him to.

'I can't believe that.' Artie leant back against the office door and removed his spectacles. He polished them nervously on the flap of his green waistcoat. 'I can't believe he's dead. Not him. He's seen everything, lived for hundreds of years. There's more power in him than in –'

But Artie never finished his sentence. In one moment, Bertie was watching him speak, his back against the door, his spectacles flashing in the light of the lantern. In the next he was aware of a rising crimson glow in the corner of the office window, a galloping of hooves from outside, and before he could open his mouth to scream there was a splintering sound and a spray of scarlet. When Bertie did open his mouth to let loose, blood dripped over his lip.

Artie had remained where he was. But there were now two jagged antlers protruding from his chest. Blood sluiced down the grain of the horns and Bertie watched it pour over Artie's curly-toed shoes onto the floor, as freely as mulled cider pouring from the spigot of a full keg.

Artie's mouth gaped like that of a fish, and his voice was clotted with blood. Bertie couldn't tell what he was trying to say, but he knew what he was going to do.

Run!

As if to help him, Artie's hand found the antlers and gripped them. They started to shake as the monster behind them tried to shuckle off their burden, but he held on, looking for all the world like he were in the driver's seat of the guvnor's sleigh, a rein in each hand, encouraging the team on through the night.

Bertie wasted no more time on Artie. He seized the lantern and hurled it at the office window, smashing the glass. He used his two-by-four to scrape away the shards and vaulted through, landing heavily on the other side. He felt his cap fall from his head and left it on the ground as he raced back towards the secret door.

Behind him came a snort and a crunch.

He's shaken off Artie. He's coming for me.

Bertie slammed into the wall, knocking the wind from his lungs. He spun, and saw a red glow behind him. As he watched, it focused on him like a searchlight.

'No!'

He threw himself to the floor just as the wall exploded, splinters showering out in a burst that smelt of burning wood and ozone. If he'd have been caught in the blast, he would have been vapourised.

How had he learned to do that?

All this time, the freak had been mocked for his abnormality. But all along, it had been his secret weapon.

Bertie hammered his way along the wall. He couldn't remember which panel was the exit. His body hurt, but he threw it against every inch of wall anyway, trying for the panel that would give way and spill him out into the night. Behind him, the monster howled like a predator. There was a flash of red so bright that Bertie was sure it would've blinded him if he'd seen it face-on. Then there were flames, out in the aisles of the warehouse.

'Come on, *come on*,' he grunted, bouncing from another solid wall. He could taste Artie's blood on his face. And then a rush of chilled air, followed by a thump as he planted his face into the snow. Freedom! He scrambled to his feet, horrified by how red the slush had turned beneath him.

Big Nick. The Guvnor.

Artie had thought he was the only one who could stop the freak. Having seen the monster's handiwork up close, he knew none of his kind could take it on. He left the spar in a snowdrift and staggered forwards, towards Warehouse One. Attacking the freak with the two-by-four would be like taking on his friends armed with a matchstick.

Another bellow from behind, bestial and savage. Bertie bolted for Warehouse One, feeling the air temperature rise as he got closer. The building was so big – surely it couldn't all be on fire? He squinted against the blaze and threw himself towards the rear of the warehouse, where the smoke was lightest. There was a door some way down and he fumbled the handle, wrenching it and hurrying inside.

He was in a breakout room. A small kitchenette housed a hot chocolate maker and a vending machine, and there were cosy sofas and a hardwood table for workers to catch their breath amidst shifts. The interior was decorated like an alpine cabin – Bertie supposed that was how this place had started out, back when it was known as the Workshop.

The closer he was to Big Nick, the safer he would be. He could hide out in here. So long as the fire didn't reach this end of the building, he would be safe.

Bertie crept to the double doors which separated the breakout room from the interior of Warehouse One. Through the glazed pane he saw it was not the storage facility beyond, but the factory itself. Row upon row of workstations, set with tools and machinery. Back in the Workshop days, they would have used carpentry instruments to make toys. Now some of the workforce specialised in computer science and digital manufacturing so that the factory could churn out the electronics demanded around the world.

The air in the factory had a dim, sludgy look about it. Smoke from the fire had crept in; he could see it hanging malevolently like a black cloud under the beamed ceiling.

Behind him came a snuffling sound. He turned and saw a halo of red around the door to the breakout room. He was here! The freak had followed him here!

Slowly, Bertie backed into the double doors, scrabbling as quietly as he could for the handles. The doors opened on well-oiled hinges and Bertie hurried in, feet soft on the floor. He started down a column of workbenches, alert for anything that might make an effective weapon. Miniature screwdrivers, soldering irons – there was nothing of use here. He heard a thud behind him and dived to the floor.

Bertie held still, pointed ears straining for a sound. The crackle of the nearby fire and the groan of the building's structure was like a sonic wallpaper; he tried to blot it out and focus on the sounds nearby. There – a soft clopping. The freak.

Bertie began to crawl away, the flagstone floor unforgiving on his knees. He looked down to see his stripey stockings worn through. It wouldn't be long before he was bruised and bleeding. And if he didn't keep quiet, it wouldn't be long before he was dead.

His eyes were fixed to the floor, his ears straining for sounds to his rear. He nearly jumped out of his skin when he looked up and saw a clutch of workers huddled under a bench. He clapped a hand to his mouth to stifle a cry of surprise, awakening an unwanted image of Artie doing the same to him. Artie, who had died with a pair of bloody antlers sticking through his chest.

There were three of them – two women and a man. Three pairs of bulging, frightened eyes were staring at him and all three had their palms raised: *Stop! Don't come any closer!*

Bertie looked them up and down. They were technicians, distinguishable by a little brass jingle bell on their caps. The man was trembling so badly that his little bell was jingling softly, as merrily as the end-of shift bell on Christmas Eve.

Bertie waved at him, motioned to his head. He didn't know how good the monster's hearing was, but if it was as good as his impaling abilities, they couldn't take any chances.

The goggle-eyed fellow only cowered away from Bertie, as if he were the one to be frightened of. Bertie tried motioning to the women, but they were as scared as the man. At least they could control their shaking. Bertie started forwards.

'No!' hissed one of the women. 'You'll lead him to us!'

Bertie jerked his hand down, palm parallel to the floor. *Shut up!*

'Stop,' whispered the man. *Jingle, jangle*, went his cap. 'He'll see you! You'll kill us all!'

Bertie bit back his exasperation.

'The bell,' he whispered. 'You're shaking too much. Take off your damn hat!'

The man reached up to his hat. But it was too late. Bertie saw a glow of red and he leapt to his feet as fast as his aching body would let him. A moment later there was a soft *whump* as the benches in front of them all caught fire. Bertie saw a glimpse of the monster through the smoke. He was so much larger than when Bertie had last seen him as a buck. On that occasion he'd joined in with the rest of them, pointing at that big red clown nose, laughing at the ridiculousness of it. Rudolph, they'd called him. Rudolph the Red-Nosed Reindeer. Now that long, dark face was lit by that malevolently glowing nose. It looked to Bertie to be the colour of Hell's own halls. His antlers were bright red.

Bertie ran, ricocheting off the benches, bouncing off worktables. He heard shrieks and screams from behind and staggered as he looked around.

The bloke with the bell was running for his life. *Jingle, jangle*. Rudolph was closing in. Bertie watched him jump, just like the other reindeer did in their reindeer games, to clear the jumps on the racetrack. The bloke seemed to crumple as the thick hooves caught him in the back, dropping him to the floor. Bertie heard a sound like ice being crunched in a bag. *The crushing of a skull. Of bones.* Rudolph did not stop his galloping. There were splashes of scarlet from his hooves to his withers.

Big Nick wasn't coming to save them. Big Nick was probably already dead. Artie had been right – there was nothing but snow for miles around. But Bertie would take his chances on the tundra rather than run and hide from this devil. He skidded to a halt and began running back the way he'd come, vaulting a bench that had been knocked to one side. The freak had built up too much momentum; he couldn't spin on the spot like Bertie could. Bertie had a head start. He used it.

He was running when he felt the red spotlight hit him again. It was not a tangible feeling, nothing hot or cold. It was nothing he could feel physically. He felt it in his soul; this strange form of pyrokinesis used by the misfit reindeer. He let himself collapse to the ground as, overhead, the very air seemed to detonate, smashing benches and scattering toolsets. Bertie felt the violence of the blast and let it fuel him as he picked himself up and sprinted. Out through the double doors, past the hot chocolate maker and the vending machine, back out into the snow. He slid in the melted slush and fell to his knees. When he looked up, hope flooded his veins.

Big Nick's sleigh. And there was the guvnor himself, driving a depleted team of only four reindeer through the sky. As Bertie watched, he saw the sleigh swoop down and scoop up a green figure from the ground. The reindeer all bore injuries; burns and gouges. Bertie supposed they had been first in line when Rudolph had snapped and turned demonic. But they were doing their best to rescue who they could.

A howl from behind him.

He wants me, thought Bertie. I've escaped from him twice and now he won't stop until I'm dead.

The sleigh hadn't spotted him yet, he was sure. It wouldn't reach him in time. It was hovering around the first-aid wagon, picking up whoever it could. Bertie wondered where it would go next – would Big Nick start again somewhere else? Or would he rally his team, muster his powers and take the fight to Rudolph? He didn't know. All he knew was that he had to survive on his own. Just for a little while longer.

Until I'm dead…

Bertie dived to the ground. The snow piled on either side of him and he burrowed into it, covering himself as best he could. Then he let his head loll, the blood on his clothes smearing the slush all around him.

You got me, he thought, as if he could project the concept into Rudolph's wrath-clouded mind. *I'm done for. Dead.*

He felt the ground tremble as powerful hooves hammered through the powder near him. Through closed eyelids he saw the throbbing red light intensify as it grew closer to where he lay. The famous nose. *We weren't to know*, thought Bertie. *We weren't to know what he would become.*

The pound of hooves slowed. Bertie kept his breathing shallow. A snort from above. Rudolph stank of musk and blood. Into how many bodies had his antlers torn this night? How many had been burned alive in his hellfire?

The stink grew stronger, and Bertie felt burning breath on his cheek. He held his own breath, pretended his very heart had stopped within his chest.

Another snort. Then –

The stench was weakening. The pound of hooves started up and began to fade. He'd done it! He'd played dead! He had escaped the wrath of Rudolph!

Bertie let himself breathe, and slowly began to dig himself out of the snow. His body hurt like nothing he'd ever experienced. He looked up to the sleigh in the sky, wheeling about as it sought for survivors below. Bertie gave it a wave, then sank into the snow.

You'll go down in history, he thought. *You survived the night. Red Christmas, they'll call it. After the red-nosed reindeer who saw red.*

He heard the soft patter of elfin feet close in on him, and a hand on his cheek.

'Are you alive?' said a female voice.

Bertie struggled up again.

'Yes,' he muttered. 'Just. I played dead. He went straight past me.'

'Let's get you to the first-aid wagon. Keep your head down. The boss will see us by the wagon. He'll pick us both up.'

Bertie let the woman support him, and they began to hobble.

'Stay strong. You've got to stay strong,' said the woman. 'What's your name? Tell me your name.'

'It's Bertie,' said Bertie. 'I work in Warehouse Three. He tried to kill me. I nearly died.'

But the woman had stopped. She let go of Bertie and stood back. Bertie recognised that face.

'Tillie?'

'You.' Tillie's face was full of anger. 'It's you. You would have assaulted me in that warehouse if I hadn't run. You might have killed me, for all I know. You... you...'

'No,' whispered Bertie. He pointed behind Tillie. 'No. Not now. Got to get away...'

The red glow. It was back. Tillie looked behind her. Even the blush in her cheeks was gone now, so pale was she. She looked back at Bertie.

'I've got to get away,' she said. She stepped closer. 'But not you. You're staying right here.'

Before Bertie could move, she lashed out. A swift kick to the side of his knee. He crumpled into a heap.

'Merry Christmas,' she spat. Then she turned and ran.

Bertie looked up. The red light was growing closer. He heard Rudolph's angry howl, half bellow, half sorrowful scream. The thunder of hooves filled his ears. And the last thing he felt was a feeling in his soul, a feeling he could no longer run away from. It was a red, fiery feeling.

Then Bertie felt nothing more.

A Note on the Illustrations

The illustrations in this book are the work of Neil
Elliott, an artist based in Sussex.

Neil has combined his superlative talents with a pencil
with a tireless effort to capture the spirit of the stories
his illustrations accompany. It is my pleasure to
showcase some of the additional illustrations
produced during the sessions for *The Taxidermist*.

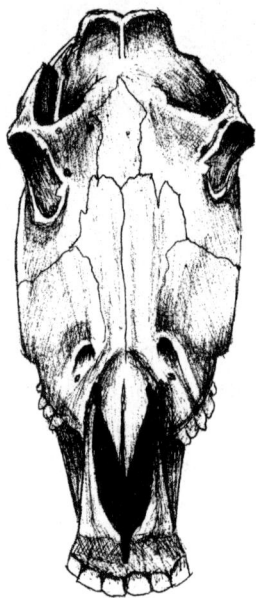

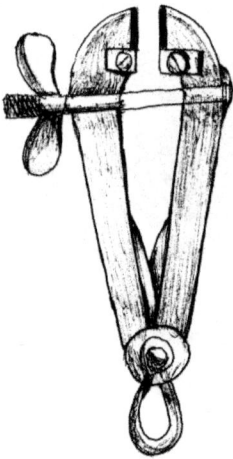

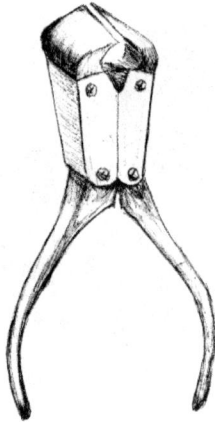

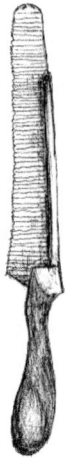

Fig 2

About the Author

Liam Smith enjoys writing quietly, drumming loudly and dressing in black. He has been known to haunt the South Coast of Sussex, bringing twisted tales and gothic performance poetry to unsuspecting audiences.

Liam hopes you enjoyed reading these stories as much as he enjoyed writing them. If you feel like contacting Liam, visit his website at:

www.liamsdesk.co.uk

or find him on Facebook or Twitter:

@HoraceCSmith

He would love to hear from you.

Printed in Great Britain
by Amazon

40227395R00118